The Boys of Bensonhurst

Winner of
THE FLANNERY O'CONNOR AWARD
FOR SHORT FICTION

THE BOYS OF BENSONHURST

Stories by Salvatore La Puma

THE UNIVERSITY OF GEORGIA PRESS
ATHENS AND LONDON

© 1987 by Salvatore La Puma
Published by the University of Georgia Press
Athens, Georgia 30602
All rights reserved

Set in 11 on 14 Electra
The paper in this book meets the guidelines for
permanence and durability of the Committee on
Production Guidelines for Book Longevity of the
Council on Library Resources.

Printed in the United States of America

91   90   89   88   87   5   4   3   2

Library of Congress Cataloging in Publication Data
La Puma, Salvatore.
The boys of Bensonhurst.

"Winner of the Flannery O'Connor Award for Short
Fiction"—P.
Contents: The gangster's ghost—The mouthpiece—
The jilted groom—[etc.]
I. Title.
PS3562.A15B6   1987   813'.54   86-7100
ISBN 0-8203-0891-9 (alk. paper)

For Joan and Clare, Rosemary, Peter,
Michael, Emily, Christopher, and John

Contents

1939

The Gangster's Ghost

Lying with his shoes off on the couch in the parlor thinking of his dead father, Ernesto got up when his mother called him from the kitchen, and was feeling his way in the dark. The lights went out when Costanza plugged her electric iron in the three-way socket the radio and electric heater were already in. Now his mother was handing him the plaster Virgin Mary's candles burning in red glasses.

"Ernesto, go down the basement. On top. Find the new fuse," said Costanza.

To his friends in 1939, Ernesto Foppa, fifteen, with his furry arms, chest, and back, uncovered in summer, and with his meaty body, was known as Bear, and he was thought to be a little slow too, especially by his teachers. He was a poor student who disliked reading and arithmetic. His hands, though, had an intelligence of their own, as untaught he rebuilt gummy carburetors, a dying toaster, staticky radios, and for $25, from Louis Perrino, disconnected the alarm at Morrie's Watches without getting an electric shock.

In the basement in his socks, Ernesto set the two candles on the old dresser, the flickering points silent metronomes dancing with the shadows. Before he replaced the fuse, something in the dresser's mirror startled him. He polished the mirror with his sweater sleeve. The faint shape seemed to take on a chin, a nose, and eyes, becoming a face as gray as the ashes he shoveled from the coal burner. The face kept developing. The red votive lamps were dabbing in rosy cheeks. Then in shock he recognized his dead father no longer dead. Now Ernesto himself was as still as death. He bolted and tripped over the box of Christmas ornaments, hurting his toes and alarming his mother at the top of the stairs.

"Ernesto? You hurt? Answer me."

With little light to guide her, rushing down as if she were a feather instead of lumpy cushions, Costanza found Ernesto on the damp cement floor, his face against his knees.

"In the mirror," he said. "It's Pa."

"You hurt your head?" said Costanza, searching his scalp for blood and bumps.

"I saw him. He's there."

In the mirror the widow didn't see her husband's ghost, only her own face made old by sorrow and poverty. Having identified Romero in the morgue, she knew that with his vanity as Rudolph Valentino's near double he wouldn't show himself now that his face was shot full of holes.

Women had been attracted to Romero, and he had often broken his marital vows, but he always came home to Costanza, for he loved only her. Besides, honor had to be accorded to his wife or his associates would've held him in contempt. The Sicilian wife was thought to preserve the family's sanctity, and could be tossed out only if *she* were the unfaithful one. She, however, should tolerate her wayward lion who had seed enough for a pride of females. But Costanza never accepted Romero's prowling.

She was regretting now that he wasn't a ghost in the mirror. She had saved up a list of grievances from nights alone in her bed. At the top of her list was Romero's foolish lack of fear, resulting in his early death for a cause paying a few paltry dollars a week.

Even though she was armed to send him shuffling back to his grave, before he left Costanza would kiss his ghostly face, just as she had when it was torn and bloodied. She ached so much for his gaiety and for his attention in bed, even to praising the excesses of her body. And she still adored the dead man.

Coming back to Ernesto and soothing her son's face with the palms of her hands, Costanza detected again Romero's high brow, his rakish black eyes, and she wondered why the vision had come to Ernesto and not to her.

"I can even touch the floor in back," said Bianca Bassano, sixteen, the landlord's daughter, as the day's light was fading. She was ignored by most boys for her big nose, but she was liked by Ernesto for her doubt that he really was slow.

"You can't," he said.

"I'm double-jointed. Watch this," said Bianca, turning on her hands by the handball courts in New Utrecht High's school yard. Upside down, her sterling silver miraculous medal on the silver chain around her neck fell into her mouth, and her skirt fell, showing her pink cotton underpants.

Before now, Bianca hadn't stirred up feelings in Ernesto. But they were suddenly there, in his limbs, on his face, in his mouth. She seemed made of bunches of the wine grapes grown by her father in the backyard. "That's pretty good," said Ernesto. "I could show you a ghost."

"Bear, there's no such thing," said Bianca, disapproving of his superstition, tossing her chestnut curls put up in rags at night, yet knowing curls wouldn't shrink her nose. She wanted to be noticed by the boys, as were her cousins Tina and Julia. Not that Bianca liked any boy more than Ernesto. Ernesto was the big teddy bear who had rescued her last winter from fresh boys throwing snowballs.

"You can see it yourself. Come down the basement," he said. "By the outside doors, so my mother, she won't see me bringing you down."

"Why she care?" said Bianca, twinkling, sensing his growing interest. "What would you do?"

"Nothing. Talk. Play cards." Ernesto was acting the dunce teachers and others thought he was. The ploy enabled him to escape uncomfortable questions, but proved to himself at least that he could fool people confident of their own superior intellect.

"If I see your ghost, Bear, will you watch me stand on my head? I can do it in the basement."

"I'll watch you," said Ernesto.

From eight kitchens in apartments on both sides of the alley, cooking smells made an antipasto for Ernesto's young appetite as they were sneaking by, bending low under the windows. He wondered if he should've gone in for his dinner instead. Reaching the backyard, Bianca pressed flat against the building while Ernesto wrestled with the double doors inclined on the ground.

The candles having been returned to the Virgin, Ernesto first tried conjuring up the ghost by striking paper book matches, while Bianca peered in the mirror earnestly, wishing it there. The matches were soon used up without the ghost appearing. So Ernesto turned on the electric light and then he ahhhhed.

"See. It's him. My father," he said, chills on his spine, but not running, for it would be shameful to be afraid in front of a girl.

"That isn't anything," said Bianca, after her detective work.

"Watch," he said, pulling his sweater from his back and polishing the glass. "See him now? Hello, Pa."

"The mirror in back is just worn out," she said. "Sort of looks like somebody, but it's just the mirror."

"That you, Pa? I see you in there. Can you talk? Something you want? You want to come back? Is that why you're there? You want your body back, Pa? It's all shot up, you know. Out in Calvary in Queens where the World's Fair is. If you want, maybe I could dig it up."

Bianca was becoming annoyed that Ernesto wasn't paying her any attention now that she had disproved his ghost. So she went to stand on her head, bracing herself against the wall, her stocking feet pointing to the ceiling. "You don't know anything," she said, upside down when Ernesto came to sit on the floor. "I know all about sex. My mother has a book. I read it. She doesn't know."

"Does your head hurt that way?" he said. "I know about sex too. We could go on the couch."

Bianca came down and, putting out the light, went to the couch. Its stuffing was coming out and it smelled of cobwebs and coal dust. She presented herself to be circled in his arms and kissed. Then he picked up her skirt. When she didn't protest, he started tugging on her underpants. They were practically glued on her waist and thighs with unyielding elastic. He was wishing for more light from the dimming small windows. It seemed to him that half the fun of taking them down was to look. But if her parents or his mother were coming downstairs, the darkness would allow them seconds to be modest again.

"Now you," said Bianca, underpants to her knees.

"What?" he said.

"Bear, take off your pants."

"What for?"

"You're dumb. I knew it. I knew you're dumb."

"I don't want to give you no baby."

"You taking them off or not?"

"I'm taking them *down*. Not off."

"And your shorts. Now come over and lie on top."

Ernesto's heart was pounding like mad and his breath was coming short. And he was sticking out when he got on top. She put her hand there, leading him to the right place.

"You have to put it in," she said.

"Where is it?" he said.

"Right there," she said.

"I can't see it in the dark," he said.

"You don't have to see it," she said.

"I can't even find it," he said.

Ernesto was slipping off the couch. Still holding Bianca. Pulling her to the floor too. There he tried again and was making what he thought was some progress. Then Bianca started making peculiar sounds. She was sort of singing a hymn, and Ernesto didn't know whether to go forward more or to pull back and put his shorts on again. The decision was made for him.

"Holy cow," he said.

Bianca said, "Oh my God. On my God. Jesus, Joseph, and Mary have mercy on me. It's so wonderful. I think I'm going to die. More, more, Bear. God forgive me. I'm going to hell. Bear, pray for me."

"I can't," he said. "I have to get up."

"We're damned," said Bianca, stretching out her crucified arms. "Like Father Valenti says, we're sinners. We made a mortal sin. God forgive us. Let's say the rosary. Then I'll do my back flip."

"I never say the rosary," he said.

"You should," she said. "It always makes me feel better."

"Eating makes me feel better," he said.

A few weeks later, on her wedding anniversary, Costanza found it impossible to get the memory of her husband out of her bed. Her desire was so strong she cried and punched Romero's pillow, and would've killed him if he weren't already dead.

In the kitchen she consoled herself with a small glass of marsala, and then another. No other man could take Romero's place. She would wear the black dress and the black stockings the rest of her life, as if she were in Sicily, not in Bensonhurst. Besides, no other man would want a woman with too much of everything, even a widow. A widow was thought to be more available to sleep with, if not to marry, by the single men in the neighborhood. She would save herself for Romero, for when she would be with him again.

After she had had another marsala, she found herself in the interior of the night with only the corner train passing every half hour. The stillness was in contrast to the storm in her soul. Remembering Ernesto's ghost and having enough wine to believe that maybe her husband really was in the mirror, she began retracing her son's steps, going in the hall to the inside stairs and down to the basement with the burning candles in their red glasses.

After a minute, at this late hour, desperately wanting him, Costanza gradually accepted the tarnished oval as Romero in the mirror, not there vividly, but smoky as a vision. "You been a traitor to me. Always I was here. Always I took you between my legs. Sometimes you smelled bad. Your beard was rough, but I took it to my breast. But now you don't come home no more. I hate you. And I love you. So what am I to do?"

In his robe, Ernesto sat on the top step, awakened by Costanza's wanderings, following her voice, unsure now if he should enter the privacy of his parents together at the mirror. He was waiting to lend a hand if she called for him, as she often did, simply to have him near, to share a moment together, to soften her sorrow.

"You miss your Costanza? You have other women there? Please don't, Romero. Wait for me. I won't be long. When Ernesto becomes the man. Then there'll be nothing for me."

Costanza kissed the glass and blessed herself, making the sign of the cross as if she had witnessed her personal miracle. At peace, at least for this night, and finally ready to sleep, she took up the red glasses and, turning, saw Ernesto there. His arms opened to her. He embraced her as a son would his wounded mother.

"I think he wants to come back," he said.

"The dead rot in the ground," said his mother.

"Pa was strong. Maybe he won't rot."

"He was stupid," said Costanza. "He liked the new suit. The car. And he had the gun. You carry the gun, you stupid too."

"A guy could make some easy money," said Ernesto.

Louie Perrino also lived on 79th Street and belonged to the same gang Romero had been in, and Louie was in business for himself on the side, pulling small jobs to supplement his low gang wages. His regular duties were to hurt guys trying to hurt girls in the houses in Harlem, and to hurt other guys who forgot to pay back loans from the gang. Louie never had trouble sleeping after he hurt someone, since the guy always deserved it, and Louie did only as much damage as to be persuasive, and he didn't hate the guy he was beating up either, as if his victim was just the punching bag at Mel's Gym.

So far Louie hadn't killed anybody. But he packed the snub-nosed .32 in a belt holster at the back under his jacket. He doubted he would ever pull the trigger, since word would get back to his mother. Louie knew she would never leave him in peace. To be on the safe side, he always kept his gun unloaded.

"Ain't nothing to it," said Louie. "We just pull up to the curb. You look straight ahead. I go ask the dame, nice like. Nobody's around, the show being half over. And she gives me the loot. Then you step on the gas."

"My mother would figure it out if I have a bunch of change," said Ernesto.

"Okay. I take it," said Louie. "You get tens."

"I don't know," said Ernesto.

"Your mother on relief ain't doing good. You have to help out. The son has to," said Louie.

"We have enough to eat," said Ernesto.

"She's in that same ratty dress. She needs a new one. Buy it for her," said Louie.

"I can't buy a lady's dress," said Ernesto.

"Look. You're the only guy I trust," said Louie. "Do this favor. I could put in a good word. When you get older, want to take your father's place? I could say you're a guy has brass balls. I could say I saw them. Because you did this job."

On Saturday morning Bianca knocked on the Foppa door. Costanza, opening it, puckered disapprovingly, suspicious of this bosomy girl. As a woman herself, Costanza immediately sensed that Bianca had an interest in her son. But he was too young for girls. For now, he had a widowed mother to think about. That was enough. He didn't need a girl who swung her eggplants front and back going to the store. Besides, he would have a pretty girl without a nose he could hang his coat on. Costanza was about to take the dollar Ernesto had earned for hauling the ashes, but Ernesto, exiting from the toilet, went into the hall with Bianca, leaving his mother behind the closed door.

"I ain't seen you," he said.

"I've been around," she said.

"You want to come down? See the ghost?" he said.

"I got scared the last time," she said.

"You didn't," he said.

"Not by the ghost. But I missed. You know what that means? God. I thought the world was coming to an end. But it didn't. Maybe I won't be so lucky next time."

"We could just hold hands. Talk," said Ernesto.

"If we could read stories," said Bianca.

"I can't, so good," he said.

"Bear, you have to try. Can't you try?"

"What's the use?" he said. "I'm going in the rackets anyway."

"See what happened to your father?" said Bianca. "Maybe you really *are* dumb. Here's your dollar."

Ernesto went down the basement and threw open the outside doors. Three days a week he hauled the ash cans up into the alley after filling them with ashes. He did it for a dollar a week from Bianca's father, who also had a younger daughter, Barbara, and wife, Berta. Mr. Bassano liked Ernesto, and since Romero's death nine months before, he secretly adopted the boy as the son he wished was his. Ernesto liked Mr. Bassano too, but when he said, "You smoke. You cough. You get sick, Bear. Don't be like your father. Go learn yourself a trade," Ernesto played dumb.

His chore finished, Ernesto went to see if his father's ghost was there now in daylight too. Leaning on his elbow before the mirror for many minutes, he was remembering his father in sleeveless undershirt presenting him with two baseball mitts on his twelfth birthday, one for each of them. Then they went out to the middle of the street early that morning and pitched to each other, Ernesto in pajamas, a few cars honking to get by. Now he sometimes played catch with the guys in the school yard, but he never lent any of the guys his father's mitt.

At first that morning he didn't see his father's face. He explained it to himself that ghosts were probably out during the day looking for work. The longer he studied the glass, however, the more his father's eyes were taking shape right before his own. He wasn't afraid now, even though he was alone with the ghost, and wondered if the ghost had something to say to him, an important message from the grave. Then Ernesto thought he heard his father's voice. It was coming out of the glass softly, the way his father spoke when waking him for school, regretting the disturbance of his dreams, but doing what a father must.

"I miss you, my son. I used to think of the days when you'd be grown up. As a good guy. Not making my mistakes. I'm sorry I won't see that. And I'm sorry I can't help you out. You have to do it by yourself."

"I don't know what to do, Pa."

"Be good to your mother. But not tied to her apron. And don't be crooked. Otherwise, you'll get holes in your head."

"You had a bad break, Pa."

"Tonight, Ernesto, I ask you. Don't go drive Louie's car. Stay home. Listen to Eddie Cantor on the radio with your mother. Louie's got a warm heart, but he leads you the wrong way."

"He's giving me fifty bucks."

"But what if you break your mother's heart? Don't go, Ernesto. Your father's telling you."

"I hear you," said Ernesto.

13

"Another thing," said the ghost in the mirror. "That Bianca. You could put her in trouble. You shouldn't do that. She's a little mixed up. But nice. She could be a good friend. So give me your promise."

Ernesto was silent for what seemed a long while. He was still caught by the eyes in the mirror. Finally, to break the spell, he said, "I promise, Pa." As he went up for breakfast with his mother, he wasn't so sure he meant it.

Whenever he went out at night his mother had to know where he was going and with whom. So that Saturday night he said he was going to the Hollywood to see *Jesse James* with Tyrone Power. With his developing cunning, he even asked if she would like to come along, knowing that in mourning she was denying herself even the movies.

For an hour, while he played pinball in the corner candy store under the elevated with guys hanging around wondering what to do, Ernesto's mechanical genius had an audience. By gently tilting the machine, he was scoring to cheers, and winning more free games than he had time to play.

At eight he said he was taking in the show. Instead he took the ten-minute walk to Lorenzo's gas station, supposedly closed for the night. Alone in the office was Louie Perrino in his pin-striped suit, blue shirt, and white tie. As a sort of greeting, Louie took his fedora from the peg on the wall and tried the broad-brimmed hat on Ernesto's head.

"Pretty soon you get one fits," said Louie. "Your head must be pretty big. Or you need a haircut pretty bad."

Ernesto's hair was black, thick, straight, and unruly, while Louie's was fine, gray-blonde, and thinning, with skin horns up from his forehead. Old enough to be Ernesto's father, but younger than dead Romero, Louie was slim and neat. He was

unmarried because his widowed mother needed him and because in his line of work, if things didn't go right, he wouldn't
be coming home some night, like Romero, and it wasn't fair
leaving a wife and kids.

"My pa said I shouldn't do this."

"Your pa? Romero? He didn't have no tongue left to say
boo. How could he be talking to you?"

"I saw his ghost. He don't want me doing this, Louie."

"It's up to you, Bear. I ain't twisting your arm. Your father
says don't, so don't. But I thought you was a pal."

"I just said he don't want me to," said Ernesto. "I could use
the dough for a suit."

"You afraid?" said Louie.

"Nope," said Ernesto.

"Listen, kid. I ain't letting nothing happen to you. I know
your old lady don't have no one else. Since you're here and
all, just do this one. I won't even ask no more."

After the second feature started, at 9:30, Ernesto pulled up
in the black '37 sedan. He was surprised at not being scared.
But his belly felt like heaving up his mother's veal parmigiana.
He wondered if his father was making him sick. Maybe it was
lucky his father was dead. He had once put his fist through the
bathroom door when Ernesto was in there smoking, and Ernesto hadn't had a cigarette again until the funeral.

Strolling over to the box office, Louie showed his gun and
said, "Please. Give me everything. You won't get shot."

Behind the glass the old bottle redhead turned and opened
the back door, handing out two sacks of coins and a few slim
packets of bills. As Louie was running back to the car, the
redhead sang like Aida. Then a cop with his tunic unbuttoned
was coming out from the theater door. Louie didn't get a
chance to slam the car door before Ernesto had the pedal to

the floor. Looking back, Ernesto saw the pistol, but all he heard was the thundering train overhead. Then Louie slumped down. Ernesto kept driving. After a few blocks, Louie half straightened up again.

"Maybe we should've listened to your old man," said Louie.

Lorenzo's was closed and no one was around, and making matters worse was Louie passed out, but not bleeding much. Ernesto didn't know what to do next. He could leave Louie in the car at the gas station and hope that Lorenzo would find him in the morning. But tomorrow was Sunday and the gas station would be closed. Or he could drive to Louie's mother's house. Louie's mother was very old and might have a heart attack seeing her son passed out from a bullet that had gone in one side of his shoulder and come out the other. Going to the hospital was out. He had learned that from his father. Doctors and nurses called the cops before helping. So that left only one place to go, even though he would get in hot water up to his ears.

Costanza could be awkward, a blimp floating in a couple of directions at once, but she was now mustering unexpected strength, looping Louie's arm over her shoulders and bearing most of his weight into the Foppa apartment. Ernesto held up Louie's other side. They laid him out on the parlor's oak floor to save the couch from bloodstains. Costanza took off Louie's jacket, tie, and shirt and held him in his undershirt in her lap. She cleaned his wounds with alcohol and iodine. Ernesto was also on the floor, away from his mother, as if to avoid her seething anger temporarily held in check until the immediate problem was solved. Louie's shoulder was wrapped in gauze and tape, but he was still out cold. And he was cold in her arms. So she sent Ernesto for blankets, overcoats, sweaters, and Romero's trousers, burying Louie in them. After twenty

minutes, sweat beading on his forehead, his eyes opened unsurely, and Costanza called, "Louie. Louie. Gangster," and
then he was awake and touching her face.

"I must be dead. You an angel," said Louie.

"Watch your mouth," said Costanza. "I'm a married
woman."

"You don't have no husband," he said. "Maybe I'll stay *here*.
You take care of me."

"What for? To see you get killed? Go home to your mother.
Let her bury you. I don't bury no more husbands."

"Sorry to put you through this," said Louie, putting on his
ripped jacket with her help. "I'll come back in a week, Signora
Foppa. To show my appreciation. I hope you let me in."

"No gangster comes in my door. This time my son brought
you. He thought you was dying."

"I like a woman with a little meat on her bones," said Louie.

Costanza was sewing her new dress. It was one size smaller. A
print, navy blue with yellow flowers. Louie was coming to
Sunday dinner again. He was the driver for Califano's hearse
now.

With Costanza's approval, Ernesto and Bianca were on the
couch in the parlor. Bianca was reading aloud a story in the
Daily News one word at a time. And Ernesto, stumbling, read
aloud the same story. It wasn't as hard as he thought it would
be. They read four or five stories, and captions under pictures.
Then Ernesto practiced the multiplication tables and Bianca
tested him. If he recited a table without a mistake, she allowed
his hand to catch her softball in her blouse for one second
before she shooed his hand away.

"My father says you can have the job in his garage," said
Bianca. "But at night. You have to study mechanics."

"I know how to be a mechanic," he said.

17

"You know only easy things. He says you can't rebuild a clutch. Or do a ring job," she said.

"If I see it once, I could," said Ernesto.

"I've decided to be a teacher," said Bianca.

"If I was a mechanic, would you marry me?"

"I would."

"Even if you went to college? And could read things I couldn't?"

"Someday, Ernesto, you could own my father's garage. Maybe own ten. And I'd keep the books. And we'd have lots of kids. With big noses."

"I like your big nose, Bianca."

1940

The Mouthpiece

Guido went everywhere with his parents to translate their babble into words others could understand. His father, Alfredo, and his mother, Sabatina, were both deaf and dumb from the complications of childhood meningitis. His parents were brought together as children in the East New York neighborhood of Brooklyn where they grew up, they became inseparable and then were married at sixteen.

Alfredo and Sabatina, as children, had learned to read lips, but never with complete understanding, and they were always too poor and too ignorant, even as grown-ups, to want to learn signing. So Guido's parents flailed their arms in the air, desperately trying to say what was stuck on their tongues, and Guido became their mouthpiece almost from the day he said his first word as a baby. He listened to other people, and then, in a series of wild noises and gestures, he relayed the message to his father and mother. They answered him in the same way. Then their thoughts and feelings came out of his mouth nicely said.

To get results from the hardhearted, Guido could also rave like a madman in a loudspeaker. He was taught how by St. Finbar's priests exhorting churchgoers to fill the collection baskets. By the time Guido was sixteen, no one could ignore his sound and fury. Then his parents were no longer shunted aside by shopkeepers or other customers.

Nearly everyone in Bensonhurst in 1940 half forgot that Alfredo and Sabatina's tongues were as pickled as pork tongues in a jar. Their thoughts were spoken with conviction by Guido. A listener could even be convinced that Alfredo Trapani, squeezed together like a clenched fist, and Sabatina Trapani, thin and shapeless, both with screaming eyes and twisting mouths, were actually speaking Guido's words themselves.

"Science explains everything," said Father Valenti. "But in the end science explains nothing. We must go back to the First Cause. We say a chemical in the body. But why for this one? Not for that one? God wants certain things, in a certain way, whether we like it or not."

"I don't think He's fair," said Guido.

"You can think that," said Father Valenti.

"So I'm never going in the seminary."

"It was *your* idea," said the priest. He was dark, short, broad, and potbellied, with a crew cut and a cigar. He talked out of the side of his mouth like a boxing fan. But his secular love, proven by thorn wounds on his fingers, was the Immaculate Conception rose garden.

"I'm sick of the rosary," said Guido. "Said it a thousand times. Still no miracles. And no call. The novena was a waste."

"You'd be a great priest. Someday even maybe wear the red hat," said Father Valenti. "But I won't talk you into it. In some ways it's a lousy life. I envy your father. And *he's* a caged animal. But he has a wife. And a son. I smoke cigars. Don't shave for days. Drink wine by the bottle. But in the morning I look at the pastor's ugly face."

"What's so good about a wife?" said Guido.

"She warms a man's soul," said Father Valenti.

"No more coming to church either," said Guido. "God's just the plaster statue by the altar. Deaf and dumb. Worse than them. From a novena, He never makes a miracle. I asked people."

"It's okay. Don't become a priest. But you can't fall from grace. I won't let you," said Father Valenti. "If you're not in church, Guido, watch your ass. Some wop priest might give it a kick."

Late on a Friday night when Alfredo received his tiny envelope of a few bills, he was told not to come to the 16th Avenue storefront factory the following Monday to work. When the women on the Singers sewed the few dresses on order, the owner himself, not Alfredo, would press them.

Alfredo and Sabatina had put aside a little money which would buy their food for the next few weeks. But their savings wouldn't cover the rent due in a few days. They needed an extension until Alfredo found other work, or was hired by the WPA, or went on home relief. So Guido was sent up the dark flight of wood stairs, sounding like a soldier with his leather heels, to the front apartment in the four-family house, to ask Mr. Frangano, nicely and with humility, for a few weeks' time.

"We can't pay the rent, but we'll get it. Don't put our stuff out. We're asking nice," said Guido, talking more for himself, his voice making ground meat of the landlord's ears.

One of the worst fears for the Trapanis, and for others on their street, with unemployment like an unwelcome aunt in almost every apartment, was having the marshal come to move out their furniture to the sidewalk, even if it was winter and snow was falling.

"Who pays the mortgage?" said Ugo Frangano, a butcher, who seemed to have acquired the facial features and the body parts of the pigs, calves, and lambs he slaughtered in the yard behind his butcher shop. Those animals were brought in live from New Jersey farms and their blood fertilized his vegetables. "I loose the house," said Ugo, waving his hands, Band-Aids on all the fingers of his left hand.

"Better you *loose* it," said Guido, mimicking the landlord, although Guido knew better.

"I must have the rent," said Ugo.

"And we the rooms," said Guido.

"Two weeks," said Ugo.

"Our furniture goes, your furniture goes," said Guido. "Your door gets smashed down." Guido wasn't sure he would do that, but he would do something. Ugo Frangano shouldn't be allowed to put the Trapanis out on the street.

"One months," said Ugo, a little worried about Guido's threat, but Guido was only a boy, and not a very big boy at that.

"The old man has the lot. He goes in 6:30," said Tonino. "So we go pick his tomatoes. And peppers. Pick a bushel. Maybe two. Juicy tomatoes."

Older and taller, Tonino Aiello was Guido's best friend. Tonino's first thoughts every morning were of mischief for sport and danger, and often Guido was included. Guido contributed to their friendship his stories, sometimes hammed up for a laugh, of adults he talked to for his parents.

"Stealing ain't fair," said Guido. "In the hot sun the old man pulls weeds. Waters with the can. He can't even stand up straight."

They were sitting on New Utrecht High School's 79th Street steps after dinner. The sun wasn't down yet, but the fresh breeze was cooling their sweat. Opposite the school were the semiattached red brick houses they lived in. On the house steps and stoops young women had bailed out of their hot kitchens to the fan of outdoors, and kept their eyes peeled on their children on roller skates and tricycles, or hopscotching. Older women, gossiping like secretive nuns, were in black dresses, in mourning for an aunt one year, a parent two, a child three, and a husband five years, and sometimes it all added up to a lifetime in black. The men standing out on the sidewalk talked only to the men and they smoked and they spat in the gutter.

"If he lived to a hundred he couldn't eat all them tomatoes," said Tonino, blowing cigarette smoke in Guido's face since he wouldn't steal the tomatoes.

"His wife makes sauce. Sells it in jars, for the people who don't make it," said Guido. "That's how they live. He grows tomatoes. She cooks them. He's too old to get a job, and they don't have no kids helping out."

"I bet your mother, with your father laid off, would like some fresh tomatoes," said Tonino. "And green peppers. For stuffed peppers."

"You'll go to hell," said Guido.

"Go be a sissy priest," said Tonino. "You ain't got no guts."

Guido took Tonino's cigarette from his two fingers. He puffed it, then gave it back and said, "I might even tell the old man you're the guy who stole his tomatoes. So if I was you, I wouldn't. I hear, to scare the birds, he's got a shotgun."

Alfredo was hindered from getting another job, not only by the Depression and his own lack of skills, but also by his dead ears and useless tongue. After weeks of frantically scrambling all over Brooklyn and into Manhattan's garment district, on subways, buses, and trolleys, he couldn't find any work. Now, in

July, even shoveling snow for two or three dollars a day wasn't possible.

In his travels, however, Alfredo had learned from other men that the WPA was hiring pick-and-shovel laborers for road building on Long Island. Through Guido, he asked in the neighborhood if anyone drove to Long Island. Very few owned a car and not one went out there. And since Alfredo couldn't afford the railroad ticket either, working for the WPA was also out of the question.

When their meager savings ran out, Guido's summer job paid for their groceries. Guido worked for the Sicilian Social Society in the storefront under the BMT elevated line on New Utrecht Avenue. Membership in the club was for men only, mostly grandfathers. They sat around and played poker and pinochle, smoked black cigars, drank black coffee, and talked only in the Sicilian dialect. Guido's job was to make the coffee and serve it in small cups, empty the ashtrays, sweep the floor, go out for sandwiches, and carry messages. When the men wouldn't be going home for dinner on time, because they were playing and winning, or playing and losing, Guido would explain matters to the wives. Guido could stand up for the men, and the men knew he wouldn't flirt with their women.

Some men carried a gun or a knife in their belts. Guido asked about those things, but the men only laughed, and rumpled Guido's light brown curly hair. He eavesdropped on their conversations and understood a little, and suspected they did bad things. But they never revealed themselves. And they were always extremely courteous to him, and Guido needed the money to bring home to his parents.

The bed was taken apart. The wood pieces were stacked on end, as was the large mirror, all leaning against the dresser. The daybed where Guido slept was piled very high with the clothes from their closets. Lamps, chests, tables, pots, and dishes were out on the sidewalk. Books, papers, crucifixes, religious pictures, shoes, old Christmas cards, palm fronds, forks, spoons, an assortment of other things were all in a heap in the middle of their faded rug.

Sabatina was crying as an ape would cry if it could, not with sobs and tears but with primitive beastly sounds. When Guido arrived, he immediately understood the meaning of his mother's inhuman noises.

The Trapanis actually had had a month and a half without rent before Ugo and his brother, Felipe, with the marshal lending a hand, moved out the Trapani belongings, on the very day that Alfredo finally accepted the idea of home relief and shamefully went downtown to apply. Their few pieces of furniture, scratched and with coffee rings, and their belongings, rags really, were now blocking the sidewalk, attracting neighborhood children who leered as if a terrible sin were being committed in public.

When the men of the neighborhood arrived home after their own futile or productive efforts to earn a few dollars, streaming down from the elevated at the corner of 79th, their curses and waved fists, and those of their wives who left their apartments, were directed at the Franganos.

To avoid that abuse, Ugo, childless, sent his wife, Tessie, to the double feature at the Hollywood Theater, which gave dishes to women weeknights. Tessie already had a service for five stacked up. Then Ugo and Felipe went to Ugo's butcher shop with two bottles of red wine, salami, and bread.

Guido, as his mother's protector, normal for a boy of his age, but more so for him because he was her voice, fell to his knees, embedded his face in the two slats of her lap, and wept too. His assumed manliness was crumbling into childhood again. Guido felt helpless to comfort his mother, and helpless to haul their belongings back inside, where their apartment door was boarded over to protect against such arrogance, which Ugo believed Guido was certainly capable of.

Then Alfredo came home. So willing to clean toilets or dig ditches, he had believed some lowly job would be his, and his family wouldn't be dispossessed, but every job was coveted like life itself. If only he had applied for relief sooner, he might have the money for the rent, but their first check wouldn't arrive for weeks now. Alfredo couldn't cry. After a dazed moment, he repeatedly struck his head on the headboard to exorcise the devil from his mind before he hurt someone. Then neighbors embraced Alfredo, offering him a room in their apartment for his family for the night.

Guido swept the floor in the men's club as it had seldom been swept before. He even swept down the webs in the corners, previously left undisturbed for the spiders to go on living, but no longer.

Guido's face had long ago lost its adolescent tenderness. His was a young man's face, purposeful, energetic, narrow and sharp-edged like a fish's, with a strong slender nose joining the plane of his pointed chin. In his eyes and mouth ordinarily was a fire, now extinguished, and even his skin was unnaturally ashy. The old men noticed the absence of Guido's voice, pleasurable to them, as evidence that someday he would be one of them, a strong man. Although Guido was there in body, the old men were missing him from their lives.

One of them, Mr. Fazio, the size of a door, who, in a doorway, had to bend his head and go sideways, and was baldheaded with a giant meatball face, said, "You have your life, Guido. Mine is finished. Whatever is bad, tomorrow is better. Spit on the floor. Pick up your head."

"I can't," said Guido.

"You tell me," said Mr. Fazio. "I tell you how to fix."

"Ugo put us out," said Guido. "We have no place to go."

The old man scratched his scalp. "Your father, he has no money?"

"Just what I bring," said Guido.

"I give you the loan. Twenty dollars," said Mr. Fazio. "You pay me back. A nickel a month. No interest. Your father—he gets some rooms for twenty dollars. Take it. Now maybe you sing. Listen to me. Then you *O-sol-e-mi-o sta-nfronte-a-te!*"

The money in his pocket, Guido was on his way to Ugo's butcher shop to talk to Ugo to get the apartment back. He had stayed late at the men's club in order to catch Ugo when he was closing up. Then he could talk to him without customers ordering their veal cutlets and lamb chops. When Guido arrived across the street, he saw through the plate-glass window an old woman still in the shop, so he cooled his heels. When the woman, a shopping bag in each hand, toddled out as if her feet were hurting, Guido went in, leaving his footprints in the sawdust. Behind the counter Ugo was slitting the throats of live chickens taken one by one from their wood dowel cage. Then Ugo threw the birds with their bloodstained feathers upside down in individual pails to drain.

"Get out, kid," said Ugo, putting down the knife and picking up the meat cleaver and waving it at Guido like a knight's weapon of war. "Don't look for no trouble. I have the mortgage. I got to have the rent."

"We have it," said Guido. "Twenty dollars. The rent's twenty-five. So we still owe you. We'll get the other five. But you can let us back in now."

"Let's see the twenty," said Ugo, wiping his bloody hands on the apron. He turned the bill over as if it could be a counterfeit. Then he folded the bill and put it in his pants pocket and picked up the meat cleaver again. "Now get out," he said.

"You took our money," said Guido, so outraged his spittle flew out.

"Your father owes me a month and a half. Thirty-seven fifty. Leaves seventeen fifty," said Ugo.

"You can't take our money and not let us in," said Guido, running behind the counter and grabbing Ugo's wrist in his two hands. Ugo was used to lifting carcasses, sawing bone, and chopping flesh, and he had an animal's chest and muscle, so he easily shook Guido off. Guido fell to the floor where the sawdust got in his mouth, and he spat it out.

"If you don't go, I break your head," said Ugo, fearing a little the bull in the calf daring to reproach him, standing over Guido with the meat cleaver, the flat steel surface catching the overhead electric light.

Guido backed up. He felt betrayed and angry. Fearful too. Of the meat cleaver and the aroused Ugo. For his own protection, Guido was reaching for the knife stained with chicken blood. When Ugo saw the knife in Guido's hand, his face flushed with fury and he charged Guido, the meat cleaver raised. Guido, trembling, went down. In a blinding light he raised the knife. Ugo's weight seemed to suck in the knife, seemed to pull it out of his hand. Then Ugo, smelling of sweat, wine, and chickens, was crashing down on him.

Guido thought to take the money out of Ugo's pocket, but he was too horrified at what he had done. So he hurriedly scuffed his footprints out of the sawdust. Then he ran out as if he were an escaping headless chicken.

"Take the twenty dollars," said Father Valenti, without his collar on, slightly drunk, in the sacristy. "Don't pay me back. I have *no use* for money."

"Thank you, father," said Guido. "And now, for you, I want to do something. Go in the priesthood."

"Don't do it *for me*," said the priest. "That's a heavy responsibility."

"I thought you'd like the idea," said Guido. "Anyway, I'm doing it."

"I always felt *you* had the calling," said the priest. "But you're still young. Don't say absolutely. It's good you want to. But there's time."

"But who's going to speak for my father and mother when I go to the seminary?" said Guido.

"I will," said Father Valenti, sitting up, wiping his mouth with the soiled napkin, as if to show he would qualify for Guido's job.

"You'll go to the store?" said Guido.

"If they'll have me," said the priest.

"To Dr. Pilo's office?"

"Yes."

"Even at night?"

"I'll go anywhere with them. Any time," said the priest. "And give them absolution. Without confession."

"Make the papers, father. I want to go as soon as possible," said Guido.

"It takes six months, Guido. Maybe more. Maybe you'll change your mind. If you change it, it's okay," said the priest.

"You're an idiot," said Tonino, dancing in the fresh snow as they went to the elevated. "You ain't ever going to get laid. You poor bastard. Means I get yours too."

"I have the calling," said Guido, pulling his moth-eaten

woolen hat down over his ears, and wondering how he would look in the cardinal's red hat.

Tonino was carrying Guido's suitcase. Guido had his mother's sandwiches, fruits, and cakes in the grocery's Quaker Oats box knotted with scraps of twine.

"You could take my confession if I rob a bank. And you won't tell. Right?" said Tonino.

"You don't have to tell everything, even if you're supposed to," said Guido. "I wouldn't want to hear you robbed a bank. You can tell God Himself instead. He has ears that can hear."

"I'm going to rob a bank. And get rich," said Tonino. When they reached the turnstiles, he handed over the suitcase. They shook hands. Then Tonino put his cold hands in his pockets. "Maybe I'll rob a hundred banks."

"Just don't kill anybody," said Guido. He dropped in his nickel. Then he went out on the platform and while he waited for the train he prayed for Ugo's soul, Tonino's, and his own.

The Jilted Groom

Under the manly figure on the cross, Lena was lighting candles at the brass table terraced with rows of red glasses, some smoking. She was lighting five-cent candles for herself, her husband, Sam, and her son, Vito. She also lighted the wick of the seven-day jar candle for her crazy sister, Teresa. Then her eyes were sending smoke signals to Vito standing beside her, convincing him to kneel there too.

On his knees, Vito heard the painted wood Christ overhead whisper to him in the neighborhood Sicilian hoarseness. "How'd I get up here?" said Christ. "I could've built houses. Raced jackasses in the desert. Guzzled wine with the guys. Look at me. My hands. My feet. They're killing me. It's cold. I have a thirst. And what if? If I just made it *all up?* What a laugh. Listen, Vito Conti, you could be a carpenter. My box of tools you could have cheap."

Then his mother's elbow told Vito it was time to go. Blessing themselves, they went to the center aisle where they bent a knee to the Host on the altar and went out.

Two pretty girls in long frothy dresses were stopping Vito Conti, Mike Bernelli, and Guido Trapani from going up the wide stairs to the Paradise Ballrooms. Vito could have hugged the one in pink, even though her big ears with gold hoops stuck out. Her face was an ivory cameo, her hair was a long dark veil down her back, and her lips were puckered in a *fungo*, a mushroom, as Sicilians sometimes liked to kiss. Vito hoped she noticed his cleft chin, his Julius Caesar nose, his killer smile.

The boys, not invited, didn't know whose wedding it was, but Mike had the knack for getting them in. He could sell old newspapers for a dollar apiece and get rich. But he was a car thief just out of the reformatory, and his eyes always looked like he could stab somebody.

"What side you on?" said Mike.

The girl in blue said, "We're cousins of the bride."

"We're cousins to the groom," said Mike.

"All you guys?" said the girl.

"Every one of us is," he said, introducing himself and his friends.

"Sue and Cristina," said Sue. "You dance?"

Vito could barely make out what they were saying, since Cristina, who looked like Saint Teresa in the picture put up on the wall in his bedroom by his mother, was filling up his brain. They all went upstairs. Then Mike took Sue's hand and she was putty in his arms as they waltzed with the crowd in the ballroom fringed with tables and chairs that looked like the lace of a giant doily. When Cristina went in the ballroom too, Vito thought she was lost to him forever. But she came back with another girl not as pretty. In the hall, before his friend Guido could take Cristina for himself, Vito grabbed her hand and led her to where kids were throwing sandwiches. He told the kids, "Be good, before you get a kick," and they behaved.

"I didn't see you at the engagement," said Cristina.

"I didn't go," he said.

"He was lying you're cousins," she said.

"I would've lied myself when I saw your face."

Shyly turning away, she said, "I used to be a nun. A novice really."

"Holy cow. I guess a girl as pretty as you, God probably wants Himself. Why'd you quit?"

"I missed Bensonhurst. Now I miss the convent," she said, as if she would always want what she didn't have. Not entering the other dark ballroom, she said, "Can't we talk in the hall?"

"With those ratty kids around? Anyway, you remind me of Saint Teresa. And I want you to hear my prayers."

"God forgive you, Vito. Comparing me to Saint Teresa," she said, making the sign of the cross to protect herself from his irreverence.

Vagrant street light coming in the ballroom's cathedral windows was like candlelight on Cristina's face in the darkness, and Vito touched it and her silky hair, but she looked straight ahead as if his touch was unfelt, so then he smooched her creamy cheek besides.

Turning, Cristina said, "You shouldn't." Then, for a second or two, he kissed her lips. "Suppose my cousins come in? They'll see I'm bad." Longer and harder they kissed now, her arm around his neck. He tasted her peachy lipstick.

"I want to be your boyfriend."

"Maybe I'll go back to the sisters."

Moving his chair closer now that she was moving hers away, Vito said, "I want to kiss you again."

"Why should I let you?"

"When I saw you standing downstairs I went nuts."

"You mean that? Really?"

"You're not just any beautiful girl. Almost, the way you look, if I was saying a novena I could ask you for a miracle." He hoped that as the second most beautiful girl in Bensonhurst, Cristina wouldn't also go crazy someday as had his Aunt Teresa.

As the first most beautiful girl in Bensonhurst, Vito's Aunt Teresa had attracted boys like homing pigeons roosting on the stoops and curbs, and even when they were shouted away by her father, Dominick, the boys returned as if outside her family's apartment were their coop.

Teresa's mother, Angie, tried to convince Teresa at an early age that she should give her miraculous beauty back to God as His nun, for which He'd bless their family. Angie herself had the makings of beauty. Her eyes and nose and mouth seemed like unstrung pearls in her self-absorbed face.

"I have the cough. The consumption," said Angie, when her beautiful daughter had her first period at twelve. Angie never again got out of bed, even though her bronchitis cleared up in a few weeks as Dr. Pilo told her it would.

Jealous girlfriends, pesky boys, leering men, and squinting women all abetted Angie in her plans for Teresa, and finally, at eighteen in 1933, Teresa announced that she was going in the Poor Clares. Then guys of all ages backed off, since this Groom wasn't to be made a fool of.

Teresa's convent application required proof of her good health. When Dr. Adamo Pilo examined her, he stammered and tripped over himself, even though, at thirty-two, he had examined a hundred or more pretty young women. And he proposed before Teresa left his office. That made her laugh without stopping for five minutes, until her blue eyes looked more white than blue.

Adamo was fearless about stealing God's future bride. Calling on Teresa, he made her laugh, and brought her gifts. They rode the Cyclone in Coney Island, slurped raw clams on the half shell at Sheepshead Bay, and jitterbugged at the Copacabana. They were second half-cousins, which wasn't a moral or legal impediment to their marriage a few months later, unattended by the bride's mother.

Angie really got sick then. She swelled up with hives. But she recovered, and dined in her bed on wheat fields of pasta served patiently by her husband, who was killing her with food. Her expanding size left no room for him in bed, so he went a few doors away to the widow's bed. The widow prayed that Angie would blow up into a balloon and explode, and then Dominick would be hers.

Teresa and Adamo made love as if fire were in their veins, and he doctored less, and a few of his patients were envious and cursed their happiness, but the lovers heard only the pulse of their own fevers.

But nine months later their baby was stillborn, and Teresa knew that God was angry with her. Their second baby died mysteriously after a month, and when their third was born with a clubfoot, Adamo was refused the communion of Teresa's body. Depriving herself of his love and care, and scolded by the vengeful God, she finally broke down by screaming and tearing her hair in the street, as from there God on His throne could see more clearly her misery caused by His hand.

Teresa's absence from their home carved a hole inside Adamo's chest, as if only the wires of an imaginary bird cage held him together. And while she was mad at Kings County Hospital, he was mad at home. His narcotic pills killed even his dreams, so in his sleep he was as still as in a grave.

His modest two-dollar fee, fifty cents for children, and often unpaid, kept his patients coming, some asking how *he* felt.

Old women patted his cheek, and old men pumped his hand as if to spill his grief on the ground. A boy of Bensonhurst himself—his parents still lived on 79th—he had moved back to the old neighborhood when he found out that his prosperous Flatbush patients didn't substitute for old friends. Now his patients invited ghostly Dr. Pilo to their own homes, but he didn't go, and they brought him dishes left untouched and fruits molding on his table. But their basement-made muscatel he drank too fast, and then he screamed for Teresa until someone called the police.

Then Beatrice came for an examination to find out why she was childless after six years of marriage. Her husband, Alfonso, was eager for a son to take over his pastry shop, and Beatrice was worried that he might go to bed with the hired girl, whose name, Julia, was on Alfonso's tongue all day. Finding nothing wrong, Dr. Pilo told Beatrice to send in her husband, and later he'd make suggestions to improve their chances of having a child.

Alfonso didn't show up, but Beatrice returned with other vague complaints. Adamo knew what she wanted. But drugged and longing for Teresa, he was impotent. Beatrice came back for months. Then, the night that she was his last patient, they went to his leather sofa. They didn't fully undress. And their tears flowed together as they fumbled in the heatless match.

When Beatrice trumpeted her pregnancy to Alfonso, he stabbed her repeatedly with the broad dough knife, saying, "I can't." He had been ashamed of his sterility from gonorrhea in his youth and had suggested, all along, that Beatrice was the infertile one.

Alfonso went to the burial at Calvary in handcuffs. Adamo went too. Neither man mourned Beatrice deeply. Her husband, not knowing she had conceived for him, was turned to stone. Adamo, hungering for his wife in the asylum, had merely substituted Beatrice in Teresa's place. Only the hired girl, Julia, wept openly.

Teresa was zigzagging up the street as if to catch a fly ball coming down here or there, screaming like a cat, and yelling, "God has no heart." Cars were nearly running her down. So Vito ran to his aunt, leaving his friends Mike and Guido shooting the breeze on New Utrecht High's steps. Teresa had just been taken out of Kings County Psychiatric Ward by Adamo for the weekend at home, and she was coming to visit her sister, Lena. With the heavy traffic on 79th, other guys at the curbs left their cars in suds also to rush into the street to protect Teresa, and they spat at drivers not stopping when a woman obviously needed a man's help.

"Somebody hurt you?" said one muscled guy.

"She's my aunt," said Vito, a little embarrassed.

"Who're you?" said Teresa.

"It's me. Vito Conti."

"You're a man," she said, forgetting he was her nephew, her eyes flaming gas jets. "Get away."

"I'm still a kid," said Vito, almost seventeen.

Reassured that he was, she whispered, "Don't grow up. A boy's nice. He plays ball. And flies a kite."

Despite the explosion in her face, and her dirty dress, Teresa was more beautiful than ever now at twenty-five in 1940. And Vito, at the age when boys fall in love every day, mooned at the kitchen table while his mother brushed Teresa's hair. Although Lena too had been jealous of Teresa's beauty, and was a decade older, she had always been Teresa's best friend.

"You take what you get," said Lena. "God made you beautiful. He gave you a good husband. But you get vinegar too. Oil and vinegar. Like in the salad, Teresa. Say the rosary. You forget a little."

"It's his fault too."

"Tell the truth. You like him putting it in. I like it too. Never mind the church. We're supposed to. He didn't give you babies by himself. You did it together."

"I hate him."

"I don't want to have to raise your baby. Teresa, hear what I'm saying?"

"My baby. I have to nurse my baby."

"Let me tie the ribbon in back. Looks nice. A little lipstick?"

"No. No. He'll kiss me."

"Vito, take your aunt home. Hold her arm."

Going down 79th to the Pilo house on 16th Avenue, Vito was protective of his aunt, and proud that she was so beautiful, an angel of God driven out of her head by coming down to earth.

Pacing on the sidewalk, Adamo rushed with open arms to Teresa, but she fluttered to the side. The kiss in his eyes and on his lips wilted.

"Come in and see our Sonny," Adamo said to Vito.

In the hospital Teresa's milk had stopped flowing. She bared her breast anyway for her baby in the parlor. But when the sucking produced no milk, the baby bawled furiously. So Adamo brought a nippled bottle from the kitchen and then baby and mother were content.

Teresa had been put in Kings County when the police, called often by neighbors, threatened to lock her up if she didn't shut up, and there she had been fitfully calming down. Now, on Monday morning, still at home, she seemed almost under control. So Adamo stood apart so as not to frighten her.

He was supposed to take her back to Kings County Hospital, but he didn't.

His love wasn't divided between God and wife. It was all for her. Perhaps it was too much, thought Adamo, for her as well as for him. Maybe excessive love drove people crazy. Still, as religious people were strengthened when they prayed to statues smug with their own secure places in heaven, Adamo too was stronger with his wife before his eyes even though she was as still as a statue.

In the following weeks Teresa remained at home with Adamo. For small talk Adamo chatted with Vito, who came to borrow his books and ask doctor-to-be questions. Then Teresa smiled at Vito and asked if he'd teach her Sonny to fly a kite.

Saint Teresa's picture in Vito's bedroom was so cunningly made her eyes followed him around the room, and sometimes he was in love with Saint Teresa and sometimes she was Cristina and he was in love with Cristina.

Vito was seasonally religious, more in winter, less in spring, and not at all in summer when girls in shorts and halters inspired his dreams. Religious beliefs and miracles, men in collars and women in habits, and saints—all made up a team he couldn't decide to cheer *all* year. All that summer, when not on Luigi's bike delivering his groceries, he was out with Cristina. On Labor Day, under the Coney Island boardwalk, Cristina, panting not with passion but from fending him off, and not without some curiosity of her own but without any of Vito's uncorkable urgency, closed her eyes and gave in. Connecting painfully, Vito remembered two dogs under the horse chestnut tree unable to separate and pointed opposite ways, finally scalded and split apart by a tossed bucket of steaming water. Still, Cristina would be worth it if it came to that.

She then proclaimed to all that Vito had proposed, which he hadn't, and her mother, stopping by to see his mother, invited the Conti family to visit the Naro family.

"I'm rotten," he told Cristina one summer night, "for making you put out. You're beautiful, and I love you, but I can't promise anything. Anyway, you wouldn't want a guy who wouldn't kiss you if you had a cold. Or wouldn't do anything for you except get in your pants because he had to do something else."

"Then I'm going back to the sisters. And praying that no girl ever loves you. And praying that you won't have any babies. As I won't."

Vito thought he loved Cristina, but not enough to give her chocolates, or his picture which she'd asked for, and certainly not enough to give her something big, a proposal. Jesus, a proposal was a very big thing. He was serious about her until she was serious about him, and then he wasn't anymore, not unusual for his age, but Sicilian traditions, which Vito assumed were for the other guy, frowned on him taking down a nice girl's pants, although he could a bad girl's. The responsibility fell heavier on him since Cristina was known for her saintliness.

"She told your mother you took her cherry. Your mother said she's pretty. And smart. So she'll make you a good wife," said his father. "So now you have to give your word to her father."

"I won't," said Vito.

"You should stay here anyway. Your mother wants you to," said Sam, also wanting to keep their son in Bensonhurst, but its intimacy was also made of old ideas like a wall, and maybe the other side wasn't greener, but maybe it was.

"What'll I do here?" said Vito.

42

"Do what you have to now," said his father, never expecting his own life to be changed by a miracle. "Go say *In a few years*. Then, when you graduate, we figure something out. Maybe I take you in my taxi. For a long ride. Out of town."

Hired by Tony Tempesta to drive his Lincoln, Mike Bernelli now wore a tie, suit, and revolver. And in his own Ford coupe he sometimes drove Vito and Guido to Coney Island for the fireworks exploding over the water summer Tuesday nights into October. They had Nathan's hot dogs and tap beers. Their buttered corn came from the old lady's steaming barrel between Nathan's and the electric cars, where they went next, crashing bumper to bumper into each other like young bucks testing themselves.

"I need to make a bundle," said Vito when they were out of the cars that last fireworks Tuesday.

"You don't want in," said Mike.

"Cristina's giving me a headache."

"She could get hurt. That wouldn't be nice. But if it helps you out," said Mike.

"Out of the question," said Vito.

"There ain't no exits, like at the Hollywood, if you get in the mob," said Mike. "I'm hoping you're smart at least. Going to school, someday you could explain things. Then I could take you on my boat out on Sheepshead Bay."

"I need $500," said Vito. "Can you lend it?"

"Jesus. That could buy half a new car. I don't have it," said Mike. "Tell you what. A small job. I'd be doing it with another guy. You could do it instead. A fence I know's all set to take the goods for a couple of Gs. We split down the middle."

Guido Trapani listened to their budding plan with an expression he'd learned from his deaf and dumb parents. His eyes screamed and his mouth twisted. He was trying to convey contempt that was beyond words to would-be-thieves.

On 79th the three of them had learned that friendship required secrets that if revealed made enemies even of strangers, so Guido, even though a true believer, would say nothing. Still, Vito wanted to explain matters to his friend. But not Mike. Mike was what he was, and wasn't bothered by Guido.

"I'm taking the BMT," said Guido, and going toward the elevated he spat in the gutter as if a bad taste was in his mouth.

The rumble seat and doors of Mike's coupe were left open when they went in the side door of St. Finbar's, expecting it to be empty at fifteen minutes before closing at nine. Some ceiling lights were already turned off, but the votive lamps wouldn't be extinguished overnight and they flickered like a congregation of yellow moths. In a pew at the back, head bent in prayer, was one old man they could manage if necessary. So they scrammed down the carpeted aisle to the altar rail, where Vito bent his knee to Christ in the tabernacle.

"Why you doing that?" said Mike. "You're wasting time."

"He's in there," said Vito.

"If you believe that, you shouldn't be doing this," said Mike.

"Seeing as I need the dough," said Vito, "I figure He won't mind."

Mike opened the altar rail's low gate and they went up the few steps to the altar. The tabernacle was gleaming gold, and round like a beer barrel on end, and capped with an inverted gold cone and a gold cross. Opening the tabernacle door, Mike brought out the gold monstrance, a sunburst on a stem. It was the sacred vessel in which the Host was displayed and adored during the benediction. In the center of the monstrance on both sides was a small round glass window. Behind the window was the white wafer that was the Eucharist, that was believed to be the actual body and blood of Christ.

"You take this thing," said Mike. "It's smaller. Like you."

"I can't," said Vito, freezing, not touching the monstrance, refusing even to look at the wafer.

"You nuts?" said Mike. "I bring you when I don't have to. Now you don't hold up your end. What kind of a crook are you?"

"I don't want to take Him too. What'll I do with Him? He's in there," said Vito.

"You could give yourself communion," said Mike. "That's what it is. Just swallow Him."

Mike opened the small window gingerly, as if not entirely a nonbeliever. Floating the wafer down to the white altar linen, he then shoved the monstrance at Vito. Vito took wing with the gold vessel as if it were burning his hands. Mike was burdened by the tabernacle's weight, and, not seeing his feet under its bulk, he took baby steps. He was promising himself never to work with an amateur again, and felt like breaking Vito's nose for leaving him alone in the church. A moment before he reached the side door, the old man at the back of the church came running on bowlegs, swearing in Sicilian, and waving his clenched fists.

"Jesus. Nothing ever goes right," said Mike. "That old bastard. Do I have to hit him?"

Moving faster and less cautiously, he tripped on the threshold, and the tabernacle, spilling from his arms, crashed on the stone steps and rolled to the sidewalk. Scooping it up, Mike tossed it in the rumble seat, and with Vito gunning the engine he jumped on the running board as the car was taking off.

Propped against a stack of pancaked pillows, her bed buttressed underneath by wood soda boxes, Angie was munching fried peppers, potatoes, and eggs in a crusty roll. Food usually satisfied even Angie's sexual desires, but persistent stirrings now turned her on her side and then on her belly, as if Dominick were there to be the billy goat mounting the she goat, Angie's first biology lesson in Sciacca, Sicily. But her weight bearing down was shrinking the space in her chest, and her heart was struggling to keep beating, and then it tried to jump-start itself, but, squeezed tight, it stopped just when she thought she was self-inducing her first orgasm in thirteen years.

Returning from the widow's house, Dominick called Dr. Pilo's house, and Vito, visiting, came along, but they couldn't revive Angie. Then the undertaker and his driver loosened their ties and sweated but failed to budge her body, so then Vito, Adamo, and Dominick lent a hand, but then Angie on the undertaker's stretcher couldn't fit through the doorway.

The undertaker went for a temporary casket in which Angie was stuffed, and with the help of a sixth pair of hands it was carried out and loaded in the hearse, and at the funeral home mourners paid their last respects.

In the procession driving to Calvary, Vito was alone in his own coupe, bought with money from the burglary, the car explained to his parents as a friend's in reform school. In the Cadillac behind the hearse were Dominick, Lena, Teresa, Sam, and Adamo, and after the graveside prayers the floral hearts, floral crosses, and wreaths were placed over the lowered casket in the open grave until the mourners left.

Sobbing, Teresa accepted Adamo's embrace, and then his consoling kisses, their first kisses in a year. Her mother's soul was taken in place of her soul which she had denied Him, thought Teresa, so God now would be appeased and she could be happy with her husband and baby.

"I'm going to California," Vito said to Adamo and Teresa as they were returning to the cars. "Please tell them."

"That's too bad," said Adamo.

"You won't teach Sonny to fly a kite?" said Teresa.

"Give me an hour," said Adamo.

"You won't change my mind," said Vito.

"Then you've nothing to lose," said Adamo.

In the Pilo parlor Teresa served small glasses of marsala to lift their spirits after the burial, and Adamo and Vito also smoked.

"We have a little money," said Adamo. "I'll go to Cristina's father, if Teresa agrees. Offer a settlement. That's how it's done in the old country."

"Yes, of course," said Teresa.

"I can't take your money," said Vito.

"When you have your own practice," said Dr. Pilo, "you can pay us back."

From the sale of his coupe, Vito bailed Mike out of jail and helped to pay for his lawyer. The witness the lawyer found didn't look like a saint, nor did she have a saint's name that Vito knew of. Miss Floppy Candy. She swore on the Bible that Mike couldn't have been the thief identified by the old man in church because he was in bed with her.

Not finding the right girl to marry, Dr. Vito Conti took care of babies and children day and night, and he sent checks to St. Finbar's that would've bought gold monstrances and gold tabernacles by the dozen. When he went to Sheepshead Bay one July 4 with his tackle to fish for flounder, on the dock by Mike's boat was a crowd. Vito pushed through the fishermen and customers, fearing what he would find. It was Mike, lying there on the teak deck. He'd been shot up and was streaming bay water. Searching for Mike's pulse in his carotid artery, he said, "It's me. Vito Conti." Mike was dead, but still Vito heard him speak, as he'd heard Christ years before.

"Don't look for no will. No insurance. No buried treasure,"

said Mike Bernelli, smelling of the stale and oily water, a dead fish with his mouth wide open. "The boat's it. It's in both our names. So it's yours now, Vito. And my next place, with my folks out at Calvary, is already paid for."

"I'll make the arrangements," said Vito.

"And another thing," said Mike. "That Sue, from the Paradise Ballrooms. I should've put a ring on her finger. Maybe you could do that for me."

"He's dead, huh?" said one of the men in the crowd.

Vito nodded.

Gravesend Bay

Y ou all know this one," said Car-
mine as the orchestra struck up "Do I Love You?" Applause
rose in anticipation. Melting girls were thinking that his singing,
tainted with longing, could be the history of love.

"He's singing that for me," said Julia Albanesi, who sat with
Tonino.

"I leave him in the dust," said Tonino, Carmine's rival on
the track in 1940.

Carmine Carmellini, eighteen, hadn't studied voice as
urged by his father, Mario, who slaved over his viola. Music
had always come easily to Carmine; his voice served him well.
He'd been pampered with applause since he was five.

From his mother, Carmine had inherited the looks of the
eleventh-century Norman invaders of Sicily, Viking eyes and
hair which made blue and yellow sparks in the bold Arab eyes
of New Utrecht High's Sicilian girls. These girls were taught
by their mothers to act like virgins with downcast glances, but
whenever Carmine was singing or running or just passing by,
they forgot.

"Did fifty laps," said Carmine, collapsing on the bench.

"Don't sit. Cool down slow," said Tonino, dragging Carmine to walk on the grass.

Both were about six feet tall. Carmine's legs, longer than Tonino's, knit yards together over cross-country distances, but before a finish line, his sap depleted, Carmine always unraveled and Tonino always won.

"I'm building up," said Carmine.

"Moving your arms is a waste. You ain't singing," said Tonino.

"I'll beat you next time," said Carmine.

"You're an old lady," said Tonino.

"Edward G. Robinson starts tonight," said Julia.

Julia's mother, Agnese Albanesi, sewed dresses in the storefront factory on 16th Avenue when orders came in. In the first year of her marriage to Rudy he claimed to have asthma in their tiny cavelike apartment downstairs in the rear of a four-family house. One day Rudy didn't stop his produce truck at the market at three in the morning, but kept going. In a pileup in Detroit he was killed the week before Julia was born.

"Robinson acts Sicilian," said Carmine.

Carmine liked Julia's heart-shaped face and bow mouth. She was one of the prettiest girls in school, didn't giggle, and looked sad, which got his sympathy.

"You can't tell between Jewish and us," said Julia, serving him her provolone sandwich. "We even look alike. Except *you're* different."

"I'm not inside," said Carmine. They were sitting on the grass oval inside the cinder track. "I get a kiss for dessert?"

"Mom's cookies," said Julia.

Julia made Carmine's lunch every school day, knitted his pullover, wrote him notes, and in her morning and evening prayers asked for Carmine's love.

"Let's go under the stairs," said Carmine.

50

Julia gave him her saucy red kisses, but he resisted the cookies under her clothes. He wanted to be in the chorus of angels eventually, and not a roasting chestnut, having gotten his religion, like his eyes and hair, from his mother.

Carmine and Julia went to the Hollywood once a week, held hands in the dark, then went for ice cream sundaes. If the weather was warm and the night late, he'd sing an Italian ballad in the school yard, and Julia would think his voice was the fallen angel's leading her into temptation. She would even put his picture on her dresser in place of the Sacred Heart, though over that blasphemous thought she chewed her nails.

Other boys jostled to sniff Julia's neck and rub against her hip, but she was so absorbed in Carmine she couldn't see anyone else. She kept his kisses in her diary, and some days lived only remembering them, especially as he was now running during lunch. Then she didn't eat lunch at all, and was soon swimming in her dress, and one day Carmine noticed her raw and bloody wrists. Skin from each wrist was missing like an absent watchband.

"Jesus. What happened?"

"I bite my wrists."

"That's crazy."

"The doctor says I'm nervous."

"About what?"

"It's a secret."

"Look, Julia. Everything works out. You don't have to be nervous."

"I'm really not," she said. "I'm biting them for a reason."

"Don't you have bandages?"

"I took them off."

"You have to stop."

"You can't make me."

"We won't go to the show."

"Then I'll kill myself."

"Quit it for me, Julia."

"That's the reason I'm doing it, Carmine."

"You could sing Verdi at the Met," said first violinist Patricia Schneck, her rosy face in the long vase of her neck.

Carmine and Patricia eyed each other like forbidden fruit. Sicilian students mixed agreeably with Jewish students who were in the majority at New Utrecht. The other's culture was approved of at home, but falling for it would bring their families' wrath, if not God's, down on their heads.

"I'd take voice if you taught it," said Carmine.

Patricia always seemed about to be captured by the crowd or another boy, so Carmine sought her out and he didn't let her get away. Sometimes he was in near panic, his lips drying and face flushing as if he'd run ten miles. He focused on no one else, phoning every night as if he didn't see her every day. That he was wild about her was infecting her with a wonderful illness of becoming wild about him, and they often laughed together like maniacs.

"You can't walk me home," she said as they left the April Festival.

Carmine stayed at her side in the crowd going up 79th Street. Ahead was the BMT elevated train and in the street below it the trolley car that she would take. Some of the guys stopped off at the candy store for "looseys," Camels and Chesterfields at a penny each, but Carmine was saving his breath for running and singing.

"Let's go down to the bay," he said. "They're making a new beach."

"I'm sorry," said Patricia. "I've French to read."

"Me too," he said.

"Gentiles should be with Gentiles. I'm not."

"Who cares?"

"Doesn't your father?"

"He doesn't."

"Your mother, then?"

"I'm not some kid does what his mother says."

The next afternoon and the next, Carmine asked her again to go to Gravesend Bay. Then Patricia stopped hearing the objection her father would make, and went. It was what she wanted to do all along. Steered by muscled men, the tractors coughed like old smokers as they pushed the bay back into the Atlantic by dumping in sand castles and boulders at the water's edge, turning on steel ribbon feet behind a fresh load. Tasting the salty air, Carmine carrying their books, they slogged through sand, holding hands. Midway on the new beach, laughing from exhaustion, they dropped, entertained by the whitecaps. Their kiss was small and fragile, as if breakable in two at any moment, but they were careful with it.

"Don't see anyone else," said Carmine.

"You have Julia."

"We stopped going out."

"We couldn't ever go to each other's house," said Patricia.

"It's not impossible," he said.

"You shouldn't break up with Julia. She's sick over you."

Patricia wanted to obey her father, Herbert Schneck, a decent man who gave all his work, play, and prayers to his family. But a woman was growing in Patricia, pink when she was with Carmine, absent of color when she wasn't. In the following weeks, if he didn't find her, she searched for him. They went often to Gravesend Bay, and stayed late after school.

Despite her husband's ridicule that God couldn't exist where stars were as plentiful as unanswered prayers, Anna Carmellini, believing the impossible sometimes comes true, went daily to the 8:00 A.M. Mass. On Sundays Mario kept her company at the high 11:15, where Anna always took communion, but Mario never did. Saturday evenings Anna also made her weekly confession at St. Finbar's, where afterward she said her penance.

"You have nothing to confess," said her husband when Anna returned late one Saturday night.

"You know my sins?" she said, almost as if she'd tell them, but then covered her mouth.

"True, you burn the pots, but I forgive you," he said, but Anna wasn't amused.

"Sin's in the heart," she said.

"Yours must be a lump of coal. I think you're never coming back from confession. Go to another priest."

"Father Hartigan's very pious," she said.

"What's an Irishman know about Sicilian sins?"

"I try to be a good wife, Mario."

"Tell me your sins, Anna. I forgive you better than the priest."

"Only God forgives. I want to offer my hair as a sacrifice."

"Your beautiful hair?" he said, shaking his head. "If there's a God, He'll cry like a baby."

"For the feast of Santa Lucia," she said. "And carry a candle and walk on my knees."

"That's for witches. Let's go to bed. I kiss your belly. Wherever you feel sin."

"We can't two more days. The cycle," she said. "But play your viola. I want to hear. While I say the rosary."

His viola, two violins, and a cello were in a string quartet. Their musica da camera made them famous on Manhattan's Upper East Side, but infrequent performances earned them little. Still, day and night, Mario crossed catgut with horse-hair.

Haydn's Opus 33 rose from Mario's viola as from the bottom of the sea. He nodded to his instrument, caught in the ebb and flow of the music as Anna wished she could be caught up in religion.

Alone in their bedroom, Anna heard Mario's viola in the parlor, clever, graceful, and imaginative, but distant too, touching only her ears. Instead of his music, she preferred Carmine's singing, especially her favorite song at a family cele-bration, "La Donna è Mobile," which brought tears to her eyes.

Father Hartigan said God would give her peace, she should pray and make small sacrifices, though not her hair. "God forbid," he said.

After Mass one Thursday morning Anna met Father Har-tigan in the school yard. Lined-up children were waiting to go in. Anna and the priest buttoned up jackets, tied shoelaces, dabbed away tears, and replaced lost or stolen lunch money as if the children were theirs. Anna's library opened at noon, and the priest was pleased she could substitute half a day for the sick nun. Her reading delighted the children.

It could be misunderstood why Anna and Father Hartigan were always together, but the nuns and other priests seemed not to notice. Anna noticed and so did he, but instead of their friendship ending, it grew. In his confessional Anna knelt for hours whispering with him about God and what He must be like, and of sinners to be forgiven, and in the code known only to themselves, they were talking about themselves.

One hot June Saturday night after confession the priest sug-gested they go for iced tea. Beside him in his Dodge, Anna was uneasy. Only rarely had she been alone with a man not her husband or a relative. Yet she wanted to be there. He was more than her priest, he was the man she should've had. The priest drove out of Bensonhurst and through strange streets, he and Anna wordless. When they returned to the neighborhood, he parked at Gravesend's dark and lonely beach, and still they didn't speak.

In green shorts and a sleeveless white shirt, the school colors, Carmine ran before classes, breathing with his mouth open.

Marty Katz gave him lung and leg exercises, but his speed and endurance didn't improve. Running also took place in the mind, where Carmine fell down, thought Marty, but Marty didn't care that Carmine didn't win. Marty had Tonino for that. To sweat was reward enough. Those who had to win eventually did.

"Suppose your girl's waiting," said Marty. "She's a little fickle. Just might give it to any guy comes in first. Wouldn't you run harder?"

"If it was Patricia."

"She goes for you."

"Maybe I should convert to Jewish."

"You have to ask yourself. At your age, if you'd give up a piece of your dick."

"Would I have to?"

"Marry one of my daughters in six, seven years. I married an Italian."

A spring rain fell during the night. It wouldn't have mattered on the school track banked to drain and lift, but the cross-country was taking place at six in the morning on Prospect Park's pathways. Puddles like black glass had collected on the asphalt, and Carmine often didn't jump soon enough and splashed in the water. His wet feet slowed him down even more than usual.

Carmine began too fast, thinking he was inexhaustible. Singing, he was. But even with his desire for things out of reach, even believing, despite Tonino's jeering, that he could beat Tonino, Carmine was running out of gas.

Orange arrows on trees pointed to paths. Through the trees Carmine glimpsed the lake still and gray. The park was chosen for the absence of people going to the zoo or rowing at this early hour. By the boathouse were the few spectators from participating schools. Julia's red blouse caught his eye, then her blurred pretty face. Her wave boosted him on. His team had come on the school bus, but Julia had gotten up very early to take the BMT in the dark. Carmine wished he could give her the cup. She deserved it, but she also made him feel a little guilty.

Out of breath, dripping as if from a dozen faucets, bites itching, mouth cracking, Carmine was unable to live up to his standard and hated himself. Runner after runner was passing him by as he chugged on. Under the leafing maple, coaches in whites were clumped like toadstools on the damp earth. "Carmine, your girl's at the finish," called Marty. "Run like hell." Carmine couldn't believe in the illusion. Patricia was staying home this Saturday to practice Mozart.

Jobs were scarce that summer, and many girls who graduated with Julia had to stay at home crocheting tablecloths for their trousseaus. But Julia, then eighteen, was hired by Alfonso, the pastryman, for his 16th Avenue shop. With her triangular face, she was just too pretty to be sent away. Customers would be attracted by her for gellato and ices in the heat. Alfonso was right. Sad-eyed, naturally blushed, and figure ripe, she made boys whistle and want to draw her out. If she smiled they won something that showed they'd soon be men. Alfonso, near forty and married to a young woman, looked at Julia, yearning for a still younger bride.

Hiding her healing wrists in long-sleeved blouses, Julia seemed as happy or as unhappy as always, keeping her misery as she had her joy between the covers of her diary. She read newspapers and listened to the radio with her mother, and went to the movies with her friend Bianca whenever Bianca's Ernesto worked late or went downtown to study automotive mechanics.

When she came home from the movies one moonless night, time turning invisibly, her mother asleep in her room, Julia went into the kitchen and closed the door and windows. Turning on all the jets in the dark, she put her head in the oven. She despised heaven's mysterious design excluding men from her life. Her father had run away and died. Her mother's brother, their family adviser, had become senile and was taken away when she was fourteen. Now Carmine, at the show with Patricia, was also gone from her life. Julia knew all along he wanted Patricia, but she waited patiently, hoping their religions would clash like cymbals. It could still happen, but seeing them together tore Julia's heart out. To rid herself of heartache and the memory of Carmine, she breathed in the gas.

The heavy thud she made when she fell awakened her mother, and Agnese Albanesi rushed in and began screaming from her gut. Since they didn't own a phone, the landlord upstairs called the ambulance.

Old women in black, putting their heads together, whispered and stared as Carmine went by. Fearing him, they directed their pointer and pinkie devil-horns at him to ward off the evil he could bring into their lives. A week passed before he got up his nerve and went to the hospital. Julia was pale. Her ruffled nightgown was opaque in the second layer and sheer in the first. Seeing her he loved her, but not as he should. He never dreamed of Julia without her clothes.

Tonino, at Julia's bedside, had brought flowers, unlike Carmine. Awkward at the foot of the bed, his hands in and out of his pockets, Carmine knew he should kiss Julia, apologize, offer to kill himself instead, but he did none of that.

"That was dumb," said Carmine.

"Are you smart?" said Julia.

Getting up, Tonino said, "I'll come back," but was delayed by Julia's extended hand.

"You're sweet. The flowers," she said.

"Next time you get ice cream," said Tonino, and then went out.

"He steals things," said Carmine.

"He's taking the fireman's test," said Julia. "He's brave to be a fireman."

Still a little jealous, Carmine said, "Don't let him swipe your heart."

"You going to marry that girl?" asked Julia.

For a while after graduation Carmine didn't know what to do with himself. He'd discuss with his father summer jobs he should look for, but he'd do nothing about getting them. The one thing he knew how to do of course was sing, so finally he applied to The Glass Hat in Sheepshead Bay, and was hired after a fifteen-minute audition in which he sang "The Very Thought of You," "All the Things You Are," and "Wishing."

Carmine would be going to Brooklyn College, Patricia to Massachusetts, she wouldn't say where exactly. She came to The Glass Hat often, the headwaiter seating her close to the mike so Carmine could sing to her, and she and the patrons loved it. After two weeks a talent agent said, "You could be rich and famous, kid."

Carmine and Patricia were seeing each other a few times a day, made love at night on the new beach, and called each other hourly, often with nothing to say, as if their voices hid messages. They also made many promises. That midsummer their love was still perfectly whole, a china cup without the small chips that come after years of use. The passing season and the impossibility of their love made them cling to it as something precious about to slip through their fingers.

Neither family knew. Carmine and Patricia were protecting themselves from parents who would break them up, and protecting their parents from the misery of knowing. And besides, posting the news of a love about to end seemed pointless.

On a warm Monday night when the nightclub was closed Carmine and Patricia went to their place on the sand and uncovered something they tried to bury: they couldn't ever leave each other. A first love has no history of failure, no knowledge that a broken heart survives, and they thought if their love ended so too would their lives.

"I'll take morning classes. Sing at night," Carmine said.

"I'll take the same classes and work at night too."

"Your father will be sore."

"I might be miserable, Carmine. And your mother?"

"She'll say novenas."

"I'll never give up being Jewish."

"Marrying at city hall, I'll be excommunicated."

"Will you be hurt?"

"You can touch it where it hurts," he said.

Anna and Father Hartigan grew comfortable riding around mornings, and in the afternoons she called in sick. They carelessly had egg creams in the Bay Parkway Cafeteria. They fumbled chopsticks over chow mein at Fat Choy's on 86th Street. Finally, Anna took the wheel, learning to drive within Bensonhurst, and sometimes the priest was recognized. One young woman shopping for shoes, a former nun, Cristina, saw them and phoned his pastor.

Like mannequins, they hadn't touched, kissed, or spoken a word about love. They yearned for something not even allowed into thought, were driven to be together as if they were whispered to by the same Holy Ghost who had visited Mary.

"You have to leave the parish," said Monsignor Kerry, bent and sprouting warts, avoiding the obvious questions, almost as if the same thing had happened to him once.

"It was nothing," said Father Hartigan. "But I'm ashamed."

"The nun will tell a hundred people, and each will tell another hundred," said the monsignor. "You don't stand a chance. You're one of them now. The sinners expect us to be their saints."

"Where will I be sent?"

"I'll recommend as far as possible. It's up to the bishop."

"How soon?"

"I'll call Monday. He'll need two, three days. Figure the end of next week. Next time, try the bottle, father. Won't get you in as much trouble."

Late Saturday night Mario called the church and the housekeeper fetched the monsignor. The monsignor couldn't remember having seen Anna at confession. She was at church so often she was almost another plaster statue. Surely he had seen her, but he was sleepy or drunk or feigning, and hung up on Mario before the conversation ended.

Wading fearfully into the early hours, Mario in his sleepless anguish thought of running to the church to tear down its doors. But Anna wouldn't be sleeping in a pew. Maybe she had been struck down by a careless driver. He called the police, but Anna hadn't been in an accident. They took her description and told him they would look for her in the morning.

They didn't have to. Someone found the priest's Dodge on the beach, a garden hose from the exhaust pipe run through an inch of rear-window space. The police told Mario and he woke Carmine. It was Carmine's last night in their apartment.

Carmine ran as never before, swift, at ease, without hungering for breath, without stretching for extra inches. He was the gazelle, running the miles to where police cars, ambulances, and people littered the sand.

The mask on Anna's face forced in oxygen.

"It's weak, but beating," said the man with the stethoscope.

The seat behind the wheel was vacant. Carmine heard the priest's name.

The priest had parked his car at night and they said the rosary until passing out. It was a miracle made by a mistake, as many of man's are: he'd neglected to fill his tank, and the engine had run out of gas before they could die. Father Hartigan was assigned to New Mexico's Pueblo Indians.

When Anna came home from the hospital, she shaved off her golden hair. As it grew back slowly, she seemed to be coming to her senses again and kissed Mario and took him between her legs, though she hardly said a word. Mario played his viola for her.

Forgiven by Mario, Anna then had to forgive Carmine for marrying a Jewish girl. They were invited for the first time two years later. After dinner Mario bounced their baby on his knee and asked Carmine to sing for his mother, but Carmine declined.

"He doesn't sing anymore. Not for a long time," said Patricia. "Now he runs fast. He's even faster than Tonino in their fireman's training."

1942

The Boys of Bensonhurst

The angel whispering in Frankie's ear warned him to be careful going to New Jersey, but he said, "Scram," to the pest, which the other guys thought might be a fly, and they all went up from the BMT subway to Times Square, where lights on billboards, movie houses, restaurants, and shops blinked nervously, and where even the scrounging pigeons were hemmed in. Mobs of people drifted out of step but mostly in two-way lanes, and nearly everyone, including the legless beggar man squatting and rolling along the sidewalk, seemed to know exactly where he belonged, and cars looked packed in the streets as in lots at Yankee games.

They went west on 42nd Street: Frankie, the oldest at seventeen; Nick, the altar boy; Rocco, the killer in the ring and with dames; and Gene, wild on the drums and the youngest at fifteen.

"I love this place," said Rocco, shadowboxing in the street.

"Lots of dames around," said Frankie.

Cardboard dames in underpants and bras were posted by the lurid movie houses, and live dames in split skirts and open blouses were in doorways, all looking for customers. Bells were ringing in arcades for pinball, miniature bowling, and peep shows. Greasy smoke blew from narrow shops grilling hot dogs, hamburgers, and knishes, shops which would be closed for a few hours before dawn with see-through steel gates. White-hat hawkers urged the guys to buy beers, orange drinks, cotton candy, caramel popcorn, and homemade fudge. Almost anything a guy could want was for sale.

The pedestrians were all sizes, ages, colors, sexes, rich and poor. They gawked at the hustlers and pimps who gawked back. Horns and tail pipes played flat, while loudspeakers from record shops played the hits so far in 1942. In a bookstore window the nudist magazine *Sunbathers* had on its cover naked dames with pubic hair. So the guys went inside. Frankie Primo often read magazines and books, rode on an old Harley, was secretly in love with an older dame, and didn't want to go in the Army. Of Sicilian blood, he was a little ashamed that he wasn't eager to kill Japs and Nazis. Every other Sicilian guy he knew of couldn't wait.

"You ever read this?" said Frankie.

"It must be about screwing," said Nick Consoli, who wanted to be one of the boys, and often went along, but at the crucial moment he could hold back, remembering what sin was, as he was doing now, shaking his head. "Screwing's bad for the soul."

"Everything's about screwing," said Frankie, acting the man of the world.

The man in charge crooked his finger at them, so Frankie and his friends moved to the shadowy back of the store. There the man dealt out cards face-down on the glass showcase like hands of poker. When he flipped them over, they weren't aces and kings; they were snapshots of naked dames turning themselves inside out to show how they were made. The guys got frog eyes.

"How much?" said Frankie.

"A fin," said the man.

"Five bucks for pictures?" said Frankie. "You're kidding?"

"Get *out*," said the man. "*Out*. Before I kick asses. Scummy kids."

Farther down 42nd was the bus terminal with snaking lines at ticket windows, with sitters on suitcases and hard benches, and blind-looking people hurrying somewhere, and others dragging, unhappy to go where they were going. Not knowing which line to get in, the boys went to Information.

"You don't want the Greyhound," said the colored guy. "It don't stop in Union City. You want the Madison line. It's red and white. It goes to Jersey by the Skyway."

At the first and only stop in Union City everybody got off, as if the only reason to go there was to see the show. It was almost June and the light was still out, and they all went up the hilly street, passing old brick buildings with boarded-up windows, dark warehouses where nothing useful could be kept, scurrying rats, and drunks nursing like babies from bottles in paper bags.

"Poor bastards. We ought to help them out. But we ain't got time," said Frankie, and his angel whispered her agreement.

The boys kept their eyes peeled in case a derelict should pounce from a doorway with a filthy proposition. They were a little scared, except for Rocco Marino. He threw a left jab at an invisible opponent to dare trouble to come out. But then, without being asked, Rocco gave a dollar to the old man with a balding beard and one-tooth grin.

"I got dough from my fights," Rocco said to his friends, who didn't have as much. He didn't want them to think he was a show-off.

When the crowd turned the corner, the street was in the

glaring spotlight of thousands of burning white bulbs on the Hudson Theater's marquee, reading in capital letters:

B U R L E S Q U E

"We have half an hour still," said Frankie.

"How about a beer?" said Gene Dragoni, hoping the bar next to the theater wouldn't find him too young.

"First, let's get tickets," said Nick. "If they sold out while we're sipping suds, it would be a waste. After that trip."

They got in line. But the seats weren't reserved. So instead of drinking their beers in Little Lil's Bar, bought from Lil herself, who was built like a wrestler and who winked at Gene although she knew they were all underage, they took their bottles to seats in the third row of the balcony.

The orchestra's lower half was already mostly filled, though not entirely by servicemen and other men. Dames too were in the audience, with dates, or in groups of dames together. That girls were there at all seemed to the guys a little odd. But at the back of their minds they knew things existed that they couldn't explain yet. They hoped that later on, when they weren't boys any longer, they would understand such minor mysteries.

Two rows down and over to the side in the balcony were two dames by themselves not much older than Frankie and his friends, and one had rusting blonde hair. The guys couldn't take their eyes off the dames, and the dames, not taking their eyes off the guys either, even waved first. The guys elbowed each other and thought they were easily recognizable as Romeos. They talked about moving their seats next to the dames, or asking them up to seats in their row. But they were filled up on each other's friendship and were anticipating the pleasure of other dames showing off their legs, breasts, and behinds, so for now they just didn't need these dames.

People in the aisles were still looking for seats when a guy in a white jacket and black tie came onstage. His grin was so broad it was almost a mirror reflecting flashes in code. "Ladies and gentlemen, tonight we have a *sensational* offer. The most sensational in the *history* of the Hudson Theater. Tonight we have this *lovely* box of delicious Whitman's chocolates made with *imported* chocolate. Crunchy *nuts*. Chewy *carmels*. Buttery *creams*. All for *one* dollar. Let me repeat this sensational *bargain* price. All for one *little* dollar. This special sale is from the maker *exclusively* to you, to introduce their *fine* quality. And not only *one pound* of chocolates, but in each ten boxes is a *special* bonus. A *Bulova watch*. Can you believe *your* good luck? One out of ten leaves here tonight with a Bulova worth $25 *on his wrist*. What a terrific deal. I'm buying ten boxes myself. And even if you don't win, these delicious chocolates make you *feel* like a winner. So, *please*, have your dollars ready. We have only seventy-five boxes for this *limited* offer. When we're sold out, there just won't be anymore."

"Let's split one," said Rocco, taking out a dollar. The other three each passed him a quarter.

"But who gets the watch?" said Nick, believing it possible to win one.

"We can toss for it," said Gene, since the laws of chance, unlike arm wrestling, would favor them equally.

"No watches in those boxes," said Frankie. "It's the worm on the hook."

The box had space for twice as much candy as was there, not a pound, but eight pieces, quickly chewed, as the boys shrugged off their disappointment.

Another guy came onstage in his white jacket which was a little too long. He was short and square and talked up to the microphone. "All you people who didn't win the watch. In case you won one, you *can't* be in on this. This is only if you didn't buy the candy, or if you did, you didn't get a Bulova, which *now you can get*. Really, *really* cheap. But only one to a person. I know people here want to buy two, three to take home to their wife, and to their mother. But we have to limit *one each*, since we don't have too many. It's the most *fantastic* deal Bulova ever made. For just *two dollars*. That's right, two American dollars, you get a *100 percent guaranteed* Bulova. You *never* heard such a bargain. How can we do it? Very simple. They have more watches than orders. But they couldn't get rid of the extras through the stores which sell them for the *high* price. In fact, you'll notice the name Bulova doesn't appear on the face of this watch. It doesn't want regular stores knowing how *cheap* they're selling them here tonight. In stores you pay $25. But tonight, for *one* night only, you pay just *two dollars*. The man's. Or the lady's. *Solid* gold-plated. *Genuine* leather strap. But we have to move fast, ladies and gentlemen. Only ten minutes to curtain time. So have your money ready, *please*. Don't miss this *amazing* offer. It won't happen *ever again*."

"We should get a watch," said Nick, the altar boy.

"I have one," said Gene.

"Me too," said Rocco. "But for two bucks, it sounds good."

"It's probably a Dick Tracy," said Frankie. "I wouldn't buy anything from *these* guys."

"My mother could use a watch," said Nick. "I'll get the lady's." He fished out his money. Then they all looked at the watch imprisoned in cellophane and staples. Frankie cut the paper with his Barlow knife. The watch was definitely a watch.

So Nick started winding it. He was winding it and winding it. When it didn't come to an end, he handed the watch to Frankie. Frankie looked at it for a minute and then tapped it in his palm. Then he passed it to Rocco, who shook it with his featherweight grace. Then Gene weighed it in his hand and passed it back to Nick. Gene didn't want to be unkind to his friend Nick and didn't say that the watch felt empty.

Nick was still trying to get it to run when the curtain went up and the lights went out. To the beat from the orchestra in the pit, the line of dames kicked onstage with pink feathers in their hair and sparkling sequins on their underwear. They weren't dolls exactly. The guys were expecting to see the beauties who existed in their imaginations, but instead they saw average dames, with all the mistakes Mother Nature makes in faces and figures. Since they looked so human, the boys felt slightly embarrassed, as if they were leering at their own mothers or sisters, and they drooped a little.

"One on the end's cute," said Nick.

"Too skinny," said Rocco. "But mama mia, the one in the middle."

"No," said Frankie. "The blonde."

The blonde's smile looked sincere, while the other smiles looked like something was too tight, or a snapshot in the hot sun was about to be taken. The girls in the chorus were showing their teeth as if the audience was a convention of dentists. They pranced and kicked and then they bowed their behinds to applause. Frankie thought none was as sexy as Sylvia tightening her garter in her office when once he just happened to walk in.

Then the stage went dark and the spotlight was on two hands holding a sign that read MISS SUGAR BUNS. The spotlight danced to the other side of the stage where a bride in her wedding gown danced out to a jazzy wedding march. One glove, one button, and one thread at a time was a slow boil for the crowd, and she was still in her underwear ten minutes later.

The drumbeat seemed to be in her hips and breasts where she was big, and every guy was raving. Gene, who played the drums in his school orchestra, was thinking that he might come here to the Hudson Theater when he graduated in a few years and get a job at the skins in the pit from where he could look up at dames every night until, if it were ever possible, he would get his fill.

Miss Sugar Buns was down to her hairnet bra and spangled G-string, and the guys were quiet as if words had more value now by their absence. The theater was heating up and everyone was sweating and holding his breath. The drum rolled. Poised in the spotlight, to clashes of the symbols, the stripper tore off her hairnet bra. Then her G-string. The boys thought they saw everything, but from the balcony, it was hard to be sure. She didn't seem to have any pubic hair. And it all happened so fast. But they acted to each other as if they had seen the most precious thing a man would want to see.

Altogether, they saw four comedy acts, the chorus six or seven times, and three other strippers. The last was Miss Floppy Candy. Then the show was over and the guys were almost dead from loving all the dames. They had loved even the ugly ones, which a few were, but noses, love handles, bowlegs, and buckteeth had been disguised by the music and by their dreams of dames.

The crowd moved up the aisles, and when the guys were out on the sidewalk in front of the theater their eyes lit up again. The two dolls from the balcony were licking ice cream cones, bought from the Good Humor Man at the curb. One was almost a Miss Sugar Buns herself, and the other was blonde, but not as pretty close up.

"It's kind of late," said Frankie, worried about the time as usual, and reminded by that wispy voice that strange dames could be carrying strange germs.

"Let's go over," said Rocco.

"They won't give us the time," said Nick, who thought of the pain of confessing his sins that weren't even too bad.

"What can we lose?" said Gene, who aspired to brazen acts.

Frankie for his reasons, and Nick for his, hung back, and Frankie said, "We'll go take the bus. You guys can stay."

But Nick, not ready to admit he wouldn't screw one of the dolls, said, unconvincingly, "They're something."

"They are," said Frankie. "But not for me."

Rocco said, "Go have a beer, you guys. Let me and Gene try."

"Okay," they said.

Before Rocco and Gene could approach the girls, the girls came to them. The blonde said, "It's five dollars apiece. That's the discount price if we take you four."

The guys had thought the dolls admired them as handsome young lions who stood out for their Sicilian dark looks, thick manes, and straight backs. The boys had money in their pockets to pay the dolls for their services, and they weren't cheap about spending it. But they felt insulted now that the dolls weren't wanting to be kissed and petted in their tight arms. The dolls just wanted their five bucks. "Shit," said Rocco, in a mutter. So they all got on the bus and went back to Bensonhurst.

"It's nice you let me come over. I was thinking who I could talk to," said Frankie in the hall.

Sylvia Cohen wasn't asking him inside. She was looking him over, trying to guess what he would say and what she would do with him. He didn't work for Tony Tempesta or other gangsters, but delivered small packages between them on his Harley. Frankie had swaggered into Sylvia's olive oil office unafraid of anything, but his grin said he wouldn't swat a fly, and both those things tickled her.

"Saturday night's a lousy time to call a girl. The only reason I'm here's the guy got a flat. But I was going out anyway," said Sylvia, her lipstick chewed off and her hair in a mess, and Frankie guessed she wasn't going anywhere like that.

"This thing's been on my mind," he said.

"So what is it?" she said.

"You think we could sit down?"

"Look, Frankie, just because we had an ice cream a couple of times and you held my hand once, don't mean we can hang out. You're seventeen, for Pete's sake. Everybody'll say Sylvia's hard up. And I ain't. So I hope you ain't planning on asking me on no date."

She eyed him as if he was a crook, but one who wanted to steal only a fresh baked pie, and she thought she might spare a slice if he was nice and polite.

"I was just wanting to talk. You always give me a big smile," said Frankie, now worried that he wouldn't get her interested, since she thought he was a kid even though he had a heavyweight's build. Besides, she was too beautiful, with her buttery hair and stripper's figure, to give it all away easily.

"I'm thirsty. You thirsty? C'mon in the parlor. I'll get something." She didn't leave, but instead, they stood on the parlor rug, wondering what they were doing there together.

"You have iced tea?" said Frankie.

"Last night this guy was feeding me brandy alexanders. Which I loved. And he thought he was going to get somewhere. He's an accountant. So he thinks each day's a sheet in his ledger. He's so boring. His voice comes out a word at a time. You could die waiting. Almost I could've screamed. Then I had another brandy. So, actually, I'm glad to talk to you. You're not boring, but I sure wish you was older."

"I'm sorry I'm not," said Frankie. "But then I'd be drafted."

"Sit down," said Sylvia. "I'll be right back."

"I'll be quiet so I won't wake anybody."

"Yeah. Be real, real quiet. But even if you was loud, they wouldn't hear you. My folks went to Miami Beach," said Sylvia, walking away swinging her hips.

"No kidding?" said Frankie, dropping to the sofa and crossing his feet on the coffee table. Chinese-pagoda lamps and cupid lamps were on the tables, and porcelain poodles, cats, teacups, dishes, vases, World's Fair trylons and perispheres were on shelves in the corner.

The artificial flowers and artificial fruits on two tables saddened Frankie, although he didn't know why, since they were beautiful in their own right. Before Sylvia came back, he hid the flowers behind one stuffed chair, and then hid the fruit too. He helped himself to a cigarette from the brass box on the coffee table, but when Sylvia was coming back he took his feet off the table.

"I do it myself. Except I take my shoes off," she said, slipping out of hers.

They both put their feet up on the coffee table and slouched back in the plush sofa and sipped tea. Frankie was crazy about Sylvia because she always acted herself. There was no bullshit to work through. And to find out if she would be anxious to be rid of him in a few minutes, or whether she was lonely and would talk for hours, Frankie tested her by saying, "I won't stay long. Since you're going out someplace?"

"You know what they do in Miami?" she said, ignoring his question and asking one of her own, which she was prepared to answer herself. "My mother and father? They go sit on the sand. The men talk business. Jewish men always do. The women play Mah-Jongg. They go for Christmas. And now they go in the water. I went once. Almost died for something, *anything*, to happen."

"Didn't guys on the beach come over?"

"They were old enough to be my father. I just turned twenty-two. Last Saturday. May 21."

"I didn't even know you had a birthday," said Frankie. "You suppose a birthday kiss a week late is okay to give?"

"Here on the cheek," she said.

He kissed both gardenia-smelling cheeks, and then she steered him back to his place on the sofa and took his hand to keep him in check.

"You smell good," he said.

"Holding hands is one of the nicest things," said Sylvia. "It has to be somebody you like. Then it feels right. So what's on your mind, Frankie?"

He had wanted her opinion of his dilemma, since she lived on 18th Avenue and wasn't connected to any Sicilian family on 79th Street, and wouldn't have their same ideas, and wouldn't gossip. But they were having a good time now and no one else was home, and no telling what miracle might happen. Still, he had to prove that he wasn't just making it up that he wanted to talk to her, so he told her.

"I'll be eighteen in three months," he said. "Then I get drafted. But I don't want to kill nobody. So I don't know what to do." He was surprised that Sylvia looked interested.

"Somebody has to kill the Nazis," she said.

"They should be killed," he said. "But I can't be the guy pulls the trigger."

"Are you afraid?"

78

"No more than anybody else."

"It ain't against your religion?" she said.

"No. What's worse, guys from the neighborhood can't wait to get in. Their mothers cry, but they want their sons to go. It's patriotic. We have to show we don't side with Italy."

"What does your father say?"

"I asked him. He said it's up to me. That it's bad either way. It's which trouble I can handle. My father ran away from Sicily so he wouldn't go in. He took care of my mother three years. In bed, in the parlor, where there's more light and people passing by. I watched her dying but couldn't do anything."

"Maybe you're a weak guy," said Sylvia.

"Maybe that's true," said Frankie, but he knew he really wasn't a scared rabbit, and seeing his mother dying, he wasn't even scared of dying himself.

"Can't you go work in a hospital? Instead of the infantry?"

"I asked that," said Frankie. "The draft board said my beliefs need proof. Which I don't have. They can't accept my word. And, besides, even if they did, a Sicilian guy who won't put up his hands, or won't kill Nazis, everybody figures is a fairy."

"Are you, Frankie? I heard some fairies ride Harleys. Tony says cops on them are. Personally, I wouldn't know. I met one once in Miami. He did my hair. And he wasn't so bad. My motto is, Live and let live. So I wouldn't care if you was."

"I don't know if I am," said Frankie, sensing the door of opportunity swinging open. "I hang around with guys. And we like each other. And I'm a little shy with dames."

"You called me," said Sylvia. "And when I said to come over, you did. You ain't shy."

Frankie thought his guardian angel might have followed him into the house to stand behind the sofa to protect him from sin, but when he looked around he didn't see her. He thought she looked like the nun he had for catechism when he was seven. The angel had been trailing him since his mother died. He tried burning candles and saying rosaries for years, to send her away, but she kept whispering in his ear, but at least she wasn't behind the sofa.

"I don't think of you as just a dame," he said.

"Then what as?" said Sylvia, her femininity never before challenged by any male. And while a catty friend couldn't hurt her, it was much harder to shrug off Frankie's sting. "I ain't a dame?"

"You're a person a guy can talk to," said Frankie.

"I appreciate that," said Sylvia. "But if you don't see me as a dame, you have a problem."

"It could be."

"There's nothing I can do. And it's getting late. So why don't you go to a burlesque? See how it makes you feel?"

"That's a good idea," he said.

"If you went in the Army, you might like the boys. That would be a pity."

"I like holding your hand, Sylvia. And kissing your cheek."

"That doesn't count. Let me know how it comes out."

"Any chance you could give me a test? I might be turning queer and not know it. Jesus, if you saved me, I'd respect you all my life."

"I can't," said Sylvia. "This guy, works for Tony, he's married. He's Sicilian too. And, you know, he'd get sore. He ain't no pussycat, which's, I guess, why I like him. But I wouldn't want him on my bad side."

"I see," said Frankie, crushed that another guy was in the picture. He could still secretly love her, but he couldn't compete with a gangster.

Sylvia observed his sinking face, but couldn't guess how

deep was his disappointment. She might encourage Frankie now, if not with a test, possibly with a sample. He could be a fine man someday. He could love women who all needed to be loved. He could fight just battles. Many such men were already in the service, and it worried her slightly that if she helped him he would go too. But someone should help him. It was the right thing to do. Otherwise, he could be a miserable coward, and miss the pleasure of having a woman in his bed, and sharing his daily life.

"I've an idea," she said. "We'll go in my bedroom. And talk privately. Which wouldn't feel right here in the parlor."

"You're wonderful," said Frankie.

"Don't think I'm double-crossing my boyfriend."

Sylvia put the light on. On her ruffled bed were dolls from newborns to first-graders. Frankie thought his first visit to a dame's bedroom might be an intrusion on her privacy. Her bra and underpants were on her bedroom chair, and her slip, stockings, and nightgown made a pink puddle on the floor. She sat on the edge of her bed and patted the space next to her. His heart upped its beat. Then he worried that nothing ever was as easy as he thought. Never having done it before, would he be nervous? And would his angel kick him in the ass?

"Sicilian girls ain't so beautiful as you," he said.

"A girl in a bathing suit excite you?" she said.

"Is she supposed to?" he said, faking.

"Suppose she's in underclothes?"

"I've never seen any girl like that."

"Would you like to?" She turned on other lamps, filling the room almost with sunlight near midnight. Standing a few feet from Frankie, she dropped her skirt, and then her blouse. Miss Sylvia Cohen could be Miss Double Cones.

Frankie's biological system reacted as it hadn't at the bur-

81

lesque, but he stayed icy to wait for the scoops themselves to be presented. Then he grinned. When she pulled down her underpants, he went to take her in his arms. She examined him from the outside and she was pleased.

"I think I'm in love with you," he blurted out.

"Well, that's healthy," she said, not believing it, but taking it as a compliment to her figure. "I think you're just a little too sensitive, Frankie. Which a girl wouldn't expect, the way you're built. Sensitive's nice, but we all have to grow up, and go to war, in one way or another. Now, you have to go home, Frankie."

"Don't make me," he said.

"I gave you a show and you sneaked a feel, but that's that. Kids brag."

Since she kept her lips out of reach, Frankie kissed her neck like a starved madman. Then her shoulders turned down. She was surrendering, but then, mustering her resolve, she pushed free. They stood there, he in all his clothes and she naked.

"I wouldn't ever tell anyone."

"You had enough."

"Okay, I'll go," said Frankie. "But you think . . . I'm embarrassed asking, but could I, you know, take a look? I could be sure then. That I ain't queer. I might even volunteer for the Army."

Sylvia sat on the bed and Frankie kneeled, but she was shy and kept her feet together. So he put his cheek on her thigh and kissed the white pillow that was her belly. Then she fingered his hair and closed her eyes. And he looked. Her thighs were warm petals on his cheeks. Her hair was darker blonde, curlier, and in a halo. She hummed while Frankie seemed to be praying. Then she pulled his hair, not to hurt him but to draw him up to the bed.

"I love you, Sylvia."

"I love you too, Frankie," she said, about a mild illness that would cure itself. "The nice Jewish boys I went to school with, that my mother said I should marry one, they're in the service. Two are gold stars hanging in their windows. Sometimes I cry thinking about guys I had bagels with. Not that I loved them, or even kissed them."

Frankie thought he could grow old there, holding her breasts until he died, and he thought Sylvia was the most perfect thing in the world, and that maybe women everywhere were the most perfect things God ever made. "Can we always be friends, Sylvia? Can we do this again?" And, not seeing his guardian angel in the room, he made his move with Sylvia and she didn't try to stop him.

"Only one other guy touched me," said Sylvia. "Which wasn't right I let him. But I liked him so much. And now you. There must be something wrong with me that I chose that other guy. And that I chose you."

"I appreciate you chose me," said Frankie.

"You loved me good," said Sylvia. "So I doubt you wouldn't do the right thing."

"Let's again," he said.

"You mustn't ever tell anyone," she said. "Bruno would kill me."

"I promise, Sylvia. I'll never say anything. But I'm asking you to be my steady, even though I know it's impossible. Would you?" She didn't answer, but they made love again, and were still in each other's arms, not wanting to untie the knot. It was a comforting illusion to think that one was part of the other. Then Sylvia was crying and sniffling. "Did I hurt you?" he said.

"You did it nice," she said, laughing now, tears running

down her cheeks. "Someday I'll marry an accountant. I'll have a boy and a girl. I'll get a little fat. And I'll go to Miami Beach."

"Maybe *I'll* marry you," said Frankie.

"You're a goyim. No good Jewish girl marries a goyim. You're not even circumcised." She laughed. "Maybe one of these days the war'll be over."

For a long while they lay in bed, not sleeping. Sylvia wasn't crying or laughing now, and they weren't talking, but their naked sides still touched.

Sylvia thought about the Jewish boys in the Army, about Frankie who was too young to be her lover, and about Bruno in bed with his wife. Nothing good would ever come from Bruno. She liked Bruno's looks and that he was smooth on the dance floor and sure of himself. But now she had a boy who wasn't sure of himself, and it wasn't as awful as she thought it might be, and, in fact, was kind of nice. Sylvia wasn't sure now that she could give up Frankie as easily as she thought she could give up Bruno.

With just one lamp on, and both Sylvia and Frankie under the bed sheet, Frankie thought he was no nearer to deciding whether or not to put on the uniform. But he was deliciously drowsy from love's wine, which also made him feel manly, strong, and knowing. Then he turned on his belly to sleep while Sylvia was still on her back, and he put his arm lightly around her. "You asleep, Sylvia?" Her slow regular breathing convinced him that she was, so he didn't ask again. "Good night, sweetheart," he said, and heard someone's distant radio playing love songs.

The war was in the newspapers, on every radio, in classrooms, in newsreels and movies, in letters from guys in the service, in most conversations between housewives buying chickens, workers building ships at the Brooklyn Navy Yard, and between the old men at the Sicilian Social Society. Young men lied about their youth or health to dress their punches in olive drab in order to knock out the enemy sooner.

Gene Dragoni was planning to join up that summer before coming of age. He took the elevated downtown to the Marine Corps recruiting office on Fulton Street. The recruiting sergeant said, "Fill this out. Answer every question." The sergeant didn't believe that Gene was seventeen and a half, the minimum age, but he accepted the application anyway, and would tell his captain later.

Gene went home to wait for his notice. Then, he thought, he would leave a note for his parents saying he was running away, and would go into boot training as a recruit. A week later a letter came from the Marine Corps captain. He said he appreciated Gene's patriotism, but that he had called the teacher Gene put down as a character reference and the teacher had told him Gene's true age. So Gene would have to wait for a few years. Then the Marines would be proud to have him.

Next, Gene decided to be a fighter pilot. Hearing of a Navy program that would train Utrecht graduates to fly, he went downtown again. The chief petty officer with a bunched-up old rug for a face put a nickel in the vending machine and handed a Hershey's to Gene and slapped him on the back. "Send in your older brother," he said. And after he thought for a moment, added, "You have any sisters at home?"

Gene wouldn't give up trying to get into uniform, to do the manly thing, as he saw it. He had grown up with his father's uniform, a cop's, around the house or in the closet, but he didn't see himself as a cop, since his father as a cop was often scolded by his mother for being away day and night. But the cop's uniform, and all uniforms, but especially the Marines' dress blues, seemed to bestow on the men who wore them modern-day knighthood. Rocco scoffed at that.

The uniform could put a guy on equal footing with his father, could make him as tall as a cop, and mitt-to-mitt with a heavyweight champ. Rocco didn't buy that either.

"I'll go in in two years. When my notice comes," said Rocco, but he wasn't crazy about fighting for a private's pay when he was making three, four times that with his gloves, and with much less chance of coming home in a pine box.

Some 79th Street kids, when they tried to hit a homer, or get an A, but failed, next time didn't even try, and thereby avoided the failure too. Others, such as Rocco, who was flattened to the canvas a few times, always got up to win the fight. And Gene wouldn't quit either. So when he heard on the radio that the 69th Regiment of the New York State Guard was asking for volunteers, he went to their armory.

The sergeant, a grocer in daytime, was forming his new company. Most of his soldiers so far were older guys like himself who wouldn't be drafted because they had kids, flatfeet, a punctured eardrum, or a weak heart. Still, they would do their bit in the Guard, which didn't give physicals, and would protect the home shores in case the enemy got some crazy idea it could invade. So when Gene Dragoni showed up, the grocer-sergeant had high hopes that some young blood would be coming in too.

"You're seventeen?"

"Yeah."

"Why're you joining?"

"To get training. For when I get drafted."

"You ever shoot a gun?"

"No. But I ain't afraid to."

"You sick or anything?"

"I'm an ox," said Gene, who was more like a bantam.

"Let's go meet the colonel."

The chicken colonel wasn't saying much. Through his thick glasses, he looked at the paper on which Gene had written his name, address, and religion, not required to give references this time. The colonel glanced up a few times and then went back to reading the paper. Gene thought that if the colonel didn't hurry up he would piss in his pants, partly because he was nervous. He thought the colonel knew he was too young, but was taking him anyway.

Finally, the colonel stood up and shook hands, and Gene thought it was a puny shake. "Welcome to the Guard, Private Dragoni," said the colonel.

With the signed requisition in his hand, Private Dragoni was sent to the quartermaster. That sergeant worked during the day in Macy's men's wear stockroom. The quartermaster asked Gene his sizes and loaded up his duffel bag with two sets of olive-drab fatigues for training, a khaki uniform for summer parades, and dress olive woolens for winter parades, and Gene stored his clothes in Rocco's garage.

He went to three meetings in fatigues, and marched around the armory, which was as big as St. Finbar's if all the pews were taken out. The recruits were instructed on how to strip down a rifle, clean it, oil it, and reassemble all the parts. Not only did they learn to do it, but they had to do it very fast. Gene was getting fed up with doing it over and over, and with marching back and forth.

Then the regiment was going upstate for the weekend. They would fire weapons. That ignited Gene's interest again. He convinced his father that he was going to pick vegetables for the war effort, as he had done once before as a class project one weekend.

The M-1 was almost as tall as he was when he brought it

down from carrying it on his shoulder. He got into the standing shooting position as ordered, as the other recruits did too, hoisting the butt end against his shoulder, sighting down the barrel, getting ready to fire.

"It has a kick," said the sergeant. "You have to lean into it. Cup it inside your shoulder."

"Like this?" said Gene, who didn't have much weight to put behind the butt.

"And spread your feet, to keep your balance when it comes back on you."

"I can do it."

"You men, you each got a clip. When you hear the whistle, fire at will from the standing position. When you hear it again, you stop. Even if you ain't fired all your rounds. Ready. Aim. Fire."

The sergeant blew the brass whistle hanging from his neck. The live men shot at the cardboard men against the hill. The hill sponged up the bullets that went through the targets or missed them. Gene drove the bolt forward, and then, as he had learned, squeezed the trigger gently. The rifle fired with a small explosion, but it recoiled violently, knocking him on his ass, and the weapon was almost out of his hands. Taking his stance again, he pushed on the bolt to load the chamber, but forgot to squeeze. The pulled trigger exploded the round and the rifle shot back, again knocking him down.

"It takes getting used to," said the sergeant.

"My arm hurts too," said Gene.

"Your size, you should have a carbine. But only a noncom gets it. If you made corporal you'd have it. And it ain't so heavy."

"I don't think I can shoot in the prone position now. I hurt."

"Get down there, Private Dragoni."

"I don't think I can run anymore, sarge."

"Get the lead out of your ass, private."

By the time the weekend was over, Gene had had enough of being a soldier. But he had been sworn in, as in the regular Army, and he had been at the lecture that warned against going AWOL, which could land a guy in the stockade the same as a GI in the South Pacific leaving to screw a native girl. The sergeant had put it that way to give them a piece of candy on the side. The guys puffed their chests to show they were loyal GIs who wouldn't run out on the sergeant. They also wanted to show they were the kind of guys that, if they had a legitimate pass signed by the CO, would go out to the grass huts and knock off a piece of native tail.

At church on Sunday, Gene asked God to get him out of the Guard. He was too young. He was too small. He was too bored. When he grew up in a few years, he would be happy to be drafted at eighteen. Then he would serve his country as other guys on the street were already doing. It was his duty too. He had no doubt of that, but in the meantime, if God could arrange a miracle and get him honorably discharged, he would say a novena to St. Anthony and wouldn't ever go to another burlesque show.

With all the suffering in the world, God didn't have time to get back to Gene, who was more impatient after another Guard meeting. He was lectured on how to clean his brass buttons and his brass belt buckle, polish his boots, and arrange his underwear and personal items in his footlocker. He thought he was too quick-minded to worry about such crap. He wanted to do something daring and brave, but knew now that he had to wait.

When Frankie was grinding up 79th on his Harley one evening, Gene flagged him down, but Frankie was going too fast as usual and couldn't stop, so he made a U-turn up ahead, and even though 79th was one-way, rode his motorcycle back the wrong way to talk to Gene.

"You're oldest," said Gene, "so I have to ask for some advice. I wouldn't trust asking guys my own age. They can be dumb. And I can't ask my father, since he thinks I'm smart."

"Shoot," said Frankie.

Gene winced, but it meant he'should get on with it, so he did. "I joined up, but I hate it. I got to get out."

Frankie turned his bike the legal way and got off and took off his black leather jacket that was warm in the cold wind generated by his speeding. But the jacket was too warm now that they were going to talk on New Utrecht's steps across the way. Gene told him his story from the beginning, and a few times Frankie laughed, especially since he was the opposite of Gene and wanted to stay out of the service. For a while Frankie was stumped about how he could help, but then his own birthday coming up gave him an idea.

The night of the next meeting, they packed all Gene's Guard clothes from Rocco's garage and strapped the duffel bag on Frankie's Harley. Gene straddled the duffel bag and held on and they rode to the armory. An hour early, Gene shouldered his stuff and they went in. Ten minutes later the colonel came in, and Gene saluted and asked for permission to speak to the commanding officer.

"At ease," said the colonel. "Say your piece."

"I hate to admit this, sir."

"Yes?"

"I lied when I joined up, sir."

"So?"

"So I'm too young, sir."

"You took the oath, didn't you?"

"Yes, sir."

"Then you're in the Guard, private."

"But I can't be in, sir."

"Why not?"

"I haven't grown up yet, sir."

"You're the right age. I don't think you lied. You're dismissed now," said the colonel. He picked up a piece of paper and began reading through his heavy glasses. Then he looked up and Gene was still there. "I said you're dismissed, soldier."

Now Frankie stepped up and sat on the corner of the officer's desk. He snapped another piece of paper in the colonel's face. "What I have here, *sir,*" said Frankie, "is my friend's birth certificate."

"So what?" said the colonel.

"So look at it," said Frankie.

"I don't know who the hell you are, but get off my desk and out of this government building or you'll be thrown out."

"This is your last chance," said Frankie.

So then the colonel grabbed the certificate, glanced at it, and said, "It's a forgery."

"We'll go to the *New York Times.* Show them Gene's birth certificate. And say you, Colonel Whitcomb, are holding him in the Guard against his wishes."

The colonel took the birth certificate again and studied it for such a long time that Gene was sure he would piss in his pants now.

"I have no use for crybabies in my command," said the colonel, finally. "We'll send you your goddamned discharge. And don't ever come back here again."

After Frankie slept with Sylvia that Saturday night, he called her every night of the next week. Two of those nights she said for him to come over when it was dark. He should walk, since his Harley made a racket and people watched where it went. If the porch light was off, it meant a neighbor had dropped by and he should come back in twenty, thirty minutes.

In the subsequent weeks and months they ate, talked, played games and cards together, and they went to movies, restaurants, a picnic on Long Island, with Sylvia driving her old Studebaker, and across the George Washington Bridge to Palisades Amusement Park in New Jersey, and they rode the 69th Street Ferry from Brooklyn to Staten Island. If her parents weren't going out of town, they made love in their rented room in Borough Park, and Frankie learned that Sylvia wasn't a moll even though her other boyfriend was a gangster. She was just a little too hungry for excitement and a little too sad over the war from which her fellow Jews were running for their lives. Otherwise, she was a little tough, medium sweet, and very smart, and he loved her a little more now that he knew her human weaknesses.

For her part, Sylvia learned that Frankie kept his word, that if he said he would arrive at six he did, if he said he would bring wine he did, and that he hadn't told his friends he was sleeping with her. They grew used to each other, and loved each other, and were careful that Bruno didn't find out. Since Bruno was married and, according to him, had a Sicilian wife who would roast his nuts in olive oil, he wasn't around much, and Sylvia, using her clever mind, cut back even on the few demands he did make. She slept with him twice in June (including Frankie's graduation night) and twice in July and twice again in August, and by then Bruno was making her sick.

The only thing that Bruno was doing differently was making the most of the few times they had together. But Sylvia was feeling more and more like the whore who screws for money but doesn't get paid. If she was paid by Bruno, perhaps she could go on with it, especially if she bought gold jewelry with the money. But Bruno didn't even bring her flowers, which Frankie did, from his father's garden, once a fragrant bunch of lilies of the valley, and another time zinnias with the colors of crayons.

"I'll tell him something," she said.

"It's better I talk to him man-to-man."

"Don't be dumb, Frankie. He carries a gun. He'll blow your brains out."

"Better me than you," he said, and the voice in his ear said indeed it would be him and not her.

"That's very brave," she said.

"He doesn't scare me."

"I know that."

"So I'll go have it out with him."

"You won't. That's an order."

"I don't take orders."

"You will from me."

"Sylvia, I can't let you risk your pretty neck."

"Kiss my toes."

"Jesus."

"Kiss them. You said you would if I asked. So do it."

"What's that going to prove?"

"That you love me enough to do what I say. I'm waiting."

Frankie got down on his knees and kissed her red painted toenails. Her toes didn't smell sour as his could, but of perfume, which seemed to be hidden everywhere on her body.

"I could almost make love to your toes," he said, getting up and rewarded with a deep kiss.

"The bum's a bully," she said. "So we have to play him careful. So neither of us gets hurt."

"Tell him it's over."

"He won't accept that. He'd keep after me, thinking he said something wrong, or did something. He'd apologize. Slobber over me. Hoping everything would be hunky-dory."

"Write a letter. Say you're pregnant. Going to Puerto Rico for an abortion. You don't want to get knocked up again."

"Are you kidding? With *him* Sicilian? You think he'd let me get an abortion of his kid? He'd pass out cigars. My God, I'd never get rid of the bum."

"So then what?" said Frankie.

"I could always shoot him. With his own gun. In the motel. He always signs in as Jones." She seemed very serious, looking Frankie in the eyes.

"*Jesus.*"

"After we do it, he passes out. Then I'd hit him between the eyes. He wouldn't know he got killed."

"No. No, Sylvia. *Jesus*, no."

"You *believed* me?"

"I did."

"I really wouldn't."

"Don't, Sylvia."

"Hey, Frankie, I'm not that kind of girl. I couldn't do that, take his gun and kill the SOB, even if he is a rat by trade."

"I'm glad. Killing is the worst thing. It makes us rotten as him. My father says that."

"Not that I'm saying it's right in this case, Frankie. But you have to kill rats *sometimes*, or they can nibble a person to death."

"Jesus. Don't do it. Not for my sake," he said.

"It ain't only for your sake. It's for mine too. And I just got a great idea. It's getting us out of this mess. Out of Bruno's clutches."

"Yeah? What's the idea?"

"I can't tell you yet. After I figure out all the answers to all his questions."

"You sure I can't tell him nice myself?" said Frankie.

"You want to kiss my toes again?"

"Something else this time."

"You listening to me? And not talking to Bruno?" she said.

"I'm listening to you," he said.

"Good. Later we'll go out for macaroni and clams."

For her performance Sylvia bought a nice sensible dress that came up to her neck and down to her knees and had plenty of room for her breasts. Ordinarily, her breasts were pushing against the fabric. She was just too big-busted, the shopgirls in the dress stores would say. And her new dress was also in white to look cherry. She had had a sexy look since puberty but had kept her cherry until giving it to Bruno, which was the biggest mistake of her life.

Actually, Sylvia had two plans. If the first didn't work, then she would ask Tony to get Bruno off her back. Bruno would kiss Tony's toes. Bruno worked for Tony, and was scared of Tony. And Tony had told Sylvia, who was his secretary in the olive oil office, that whatever her problem, it didn't matter if it was money or love or hate, he, Tony Tempesta, wanted first crack at solving it for her. Even though she was Jewish, she was in his family like his sister and he wouldn't let any harm come to her.

Before Bruno asked for their next date at the motel on Long Island, she asked him to have a drink when she got off. She was in her modest white dress and almost looked like a nun in the summer habit, and Bruno didn't give her the usual slap on her ass as soon as they were alone, and not getting it now, Sylvia knew her idea was working. He took her in his Caddie to The 19th Hole on the corner of 14th Avenue across from the Dyker Heights Golf Course. At the back of the bar they took the red leather booth where no one else was around.

Bruno's long black hair was combed straight back, his teeth were slightly irregular, his face was square and strong, and he still wasn't fat from all the food he ate, and he had the kind of smile that one minute could love a person to bits and the next minute could chop a person in pieces. The bad part of Bruno's smile came from his eyes, which were brown, but not warm as brown eyes often are. His eyes were like dried blood, scabby and mean, and if they weren't disguised by his smiling mouth, then the average person could feel a chill that no amount of clothing could warm up.

"I don't know how to tell you this, Bruno."

"So tell me. I won't bite."

"I got this marriage proposal," said Sylvia, very calmly. "He's a nice guy."

"He screw you?" he said.

"You know I wouldn't," she said.

"But he wants to get hitched anyway?" he said.

"Yeah. He's Jewish."

"I thought my Sicilian cock converted you."

"He's an accountant. He'll make a good father for my kids someday," she said.

"Accountant. That's pretty good. So you're quitting your job?" he said.

"Not till I get pregnant."

"I wouldn't screw up your wedding plans."

"I knew you'd understand, Bruno."

"Hey, I ain't no animal. I respect a woman who tells me what she has to do in her life. So, do I get an invite to the wedding? Like I'm just a friend from the office?"

"It' s going to be a civil ceremony. At city hall. Just us."

"When you set the date and all, you let me know. So I can give you a wedding present. What can I give to show I appreciate all the good times we had?"

"I wouldn't ask for anything, Bruno. I had good times too. But thanks just the same."

"You finishing your drink?" he said.

"I had enough."

"Let's get out of here. I'll drop you off at your house. Don't worry, I ain't asking for a last piece of nookie. By the way, what's his name?"

"His name?" she said. "He's just a guy."

"I'm curious."

"Oh. Herbie."

"Herbie what?"

"Herbie Schwartz," she said, biting her tongue too late.

"So, pretty soon, you're going to be Sylvia Schwartz. Is that the truth, Sylvia?"

"Of course."

"Well, that's pretty good for Herbie. Not so good for Bruno. But what the hell, I'm married anyway. Maybe I'll go give Marie a good screwing for a change. You know, that butterball, she gained another five pounds last month."

Frankie and Sylvia waited for weeks to see if anything would go wrong from her dumping Bruno. Then they had a rip-roaring celebration, just the two of them, at Le Petit Cabaret in Greenwich Village. There Frankie spent his money on French champagne, escargots, and calf brains in brown butter. The show had Apache dancers, cancan girls, a comedian, and a canary, blonde, small, but with the voice of a choir.

They sat close, touching hands and thighs under the table, and saying clichés they meant. They danced cheek-to-cheek on the crowded floor. But their golden hour wouldn't last. Frankie, in order not to spoil the evening, didn't mention the greetings from the draft board in his pocket. He would tell her, if not that night, and not when they awoke in the morning in their rented room with other things on their minds, then another night.

A week went by and, not being able to tell her his notice had come, he just handed it to her. She read the place, Whitehall Street in downtown Manhattan by the financial district, and the date, Monday, November 30, 1942, at 8:00 A.M., and she wept.

Frankie now had another reason to resist going into uniform: his furious and singular passion for Sylvia, equally matched by her passion. That reason, of course, wouldn't excuse any man from the service. So he had no acceptable excuse, and they both knew it.

"I'm going in."

"We could run away. Change our names. Get a forged 4F card," she said.

"I couldn't," said Frankie, and was surprised to hear his angel say that Sylvia's plan was pretty good and that he should take her up on it.

"If you go, and won't kill them, you won't last. Not five minutes. The Nazis will aim at you first. You can't go in, Frankie."

"It would be a disgrace to Bensonhurst."

"Screw Bensonhurst," she said.

"We still have fifty days," he said.

"Think about it, honey. We could set up housekeeping. Get jobs in a war factory. What a wonderful time we could have."

"I'll think about it," he said, but he knew he wouldn't

change his mind. The right thing to do, as everyone saw it, was to go in and be a soldier.

To store up on love and lovemaking, they were together every free minute. Frankie even met her for lunch a few times in the next weeks, and once Bruno got a glimpse of them. And they moved into the rented room and played house, cooking on a hot plate and going down to the basement to do the laundry. They put the calendar in the trash and lived as if it hadn't been invented.

When Frankie came home one evening with cartons of chow mein and sweet-and-sour pork, carried from the restaurant on his Harley, Sylvia wasn't there. Neither were her clothes and things. Her note said she couldn't see him for a while, but that she would explain everything in her letter when she had time to write it, and that she still loved him and always would.

For Frankie, losing the woman he loved was no easier at eighteen than it would be for another man losing his wife after decades. He brooded for a night and a day, not leaving the room. The mystery of her departure finally drove him into the street and he phoned her house, but her father said she wasn't there. Then Frankie had to make a run to Tony Tempesta's office where Sylvia was the secretary, but she wasn't on the job either. So then he really got worried and went and rang her father's doorbell. When no one answered, he went to the back door and jimmied the lock with his Barlow knife and went inside to Sylvia's bedroom. She was in bed in bandages.

"Jesus! What happened?"

"How'd you get in? You shouldn't've come here. Leave, Frankie, leave." Sylvia was a little hysterical, which was unlike her.

"I ain't leaving," he said, sitting on her bed, touching the gauze on her face and arms. "Does it hurt? How'd you get all that?"

"It doesn't matter. I'll heal. Then I'll do what I have to," said Sylvia.

"Were you in an accident?" said Frankie, who had the true explanation in his ear, but as always it was something he didn't want to hear.

"Yeah, an accident," she said. "And I don't want you getting in one too. So don't come around no more. But write me which camp you go to. Maybe I'll send you cookies, and if it ain't too far, come and see you."

"Make a list of anything you need. I'll come back tomorrow. And bring you roses. Red roses."

"You're my honey," she said.

"You ain't getting in no more accidents," he said.

"What's that mean?" she said, sitting up, extending her arm, and he came back and took her hand again.

He loosened up to put on his wouldn't-swat-a-fly grin. "You know that angel? She's been a pain. So I'm leaving her here. And she'll watch out for you."

Frankie looked around the room, looked under Sylvia's bed, but in her closet he thought he saw her. She was a frail and pretty young thing, with bright round eyes of sky, which she dimmed shyly.

"You stay here," said Frankie. "Don't leave Sylvia. If you follow me this time I'll get sore. And besides, you could get hurt out there too."

Sylvia said, "You have a screw loose, Frankie?"

"It could be."

"It doesn't matter," she said. "I made one mistake. Herbie's name."

"Is Herbie okay?" he said.

"Yeah. He just shit in his pants."

"I won't."

The next morning Frankie was a hot boiler with a head of steam that had to be let out, so he raced his Harley to the olive oil office, but Bruno wouldn't be in until two. Tony could feel Frankie's anger, so slowly Tony prodded him. Then Frankie realized that Tony didn't know the real reason Sylvia wasn't on the job, and remembering that Tony would watch out for her, he told him what had happened.

"Beating up Sylvia wasn't nice," said Tony. "You go home, kid. I have a talk with Bruno. He belongs to me."

Frankie was still steaming when he rode off. He tried to cool down by bringing the roses to Sylvia, but when he saw her bandages again his steam rose a few more degrees. Getting back on his bike, he charged around too fast and almost spilled, but he couldn't decide on a place to go, so he steered back to the olive oil office. He had to give that bully a broken nose.

He had been waiting outside the office for a half hour, straddling his bike, when he saw Bruno walking up the street. Without any planning, Frankie turned on the ignition, gunned it, shifted into first, and, speeding up, shifted into second. With his bike roaring like a cannon going off, he aimed it at Bruno. Bruno didn't jump out of the way soon enough to avoid the bike entirely. One leg was hit.

Frankie had tried to kill Bruno by running him down, but he had killed himself instead, by missing Bruno and hitting the brick wall beside the plate-glass windows of the office. His neck was broken.

Tony came out. When he saw that Bruno was still alive, he helped him inside and away from the crowd. In the back room where the counterfeit olive oil was mixed, Tony sat Bruno on the work bench and lit a smoke for him. When he returned from the front room with coffee, Bruno sipped it. Then, with a pistol that had a silencer, Tony shot Bruno in the head and put the body in an empty oil drum.

Frankie was laid out at the Califano Funeral Parlor and, in her bandages, Sylvia sat next to his father, Giovanni, for the three days that the body was on view. Gene, Rocco, and Nick were also there every day, in suits and ties, not knowing what to say to anyone. They had known Frankie better than they had the members of their own families. They had loved him as boys do each other, simply and without question, before they must turn to the richer love of a man for a woman, complicated and always questioning.

The last night of their vigil, an hour before the funeral parlor locked its doors for the night, Rocco hid himself in an unused room. Then, Gene at the handlebars of Frankie's Harley and Nick behind him in a swiped priest's cassock, they rode across the Brooklyn Bridge. Following the Madison bus on the Skyway, they arrived in Union City and at the Hudson Theater once again. As they had anticipated, the priest's cassock got Nick in the stage door when he said to the guard, "It's an errand of mercy."

Miss Sugar Buns believed that Nick was a priest, and since he was also willing to pay her $50 to perform for a dying man, she said, "Why the hell not?"

She straddled the Harley too, showing her thighs that Nick, behind her, thought were like moonlight in bottles, and with the cassock flaring out behind him like a ghost in the night trying to keep up with them, Nick was holding on around her waist as she held onto Gene in front, who was letting all the untamed juice out of the Harley and speeding in a race of one.

Nick was deciding now that he was too old to be an altar boy anymore. He wanted girls, dozens, hundreds of girls.

"This isn't a hospital," said Miss Sugar Buns, as Gene knocked three times on the funeral parlor's back door, and then repeated it.

"You still get fifty bucks," said Gene.

"What took you guys so long?" said Rocco, letting them in. "I was getting scared in here by myself."

"God, he's dead," she said. "He won't enjoy it."

"Give him a chance," said Gene, doing a practice drum roll, his drums unpacked by Rocco while he was waiting.

"He can't see so good lying down," said Rocco. "Let's get him up."

"He's too big," said Nick, standing at the casket.

"Give me a hand," said Rocco, at Frankie's head.

"Where to? His legs're stiff," said Nick.

"Let's stand him some place," said Rocco, looking around, as he and Nick gripped Frankie at each end.

Miss Sugar Buns said, "First, let's see the scratch."

"You ain't only seeing it," said Gene, taking out the money, "but you're getting it. *In advance.*"

"That's sweet. I never been paid in advance." She stashed the bills in her purse.

Frankie was a heavy and stiff lead soldier that Rocco and Nick were standing in the corner now, where they pried open his aggie eyes. To keep Frankie from keeling over, they straddled chairs at each side of him. Then, by candlelight, less noticeable from the street than electric light, and by Gene's drumbeat, Miss Sugar Buns loosened and discarded, stretching it out, peeling one garment so slowly, bumping and grinding, for the pleasure of the dead Frankie.

She stripped off all her clothes, until she got down to her

hairnet bra and spangled G-string. She wore them even under her street clothes when she went to buy groceries. And when those gossamer items flew from her body, the guys all nodded. They thought they had again seen everything she had, although the funeral parlor wasn't ablaze in a spotlight, and their eyes weren't dry, and their view was filtered, on purpose, through the fingers of Frankie's angel.

1943

Wear It in Good Health

He stuffed his pillow under his belly and the pain napped a little, but returning from his failed bathroom visit he groaned, waking his mother, Philomena, who said from the other bedroom, "You sick, Joey?"

"No," he lied.

She came to his room which he shared with his brother, Gino, who was asleep, and when she switched on the lamp she was frightened. Joey was doubled up, and she thought of her Uncle Guy's false heart attack that turned out to be his burst appendix in the autopsy.

"We have Alka-Seltzer?" said Joey.

"It has the aspirin. Not good for the stomach."

"What's better? Hanging camphor balls around my neck?" Joey's voice was serrated with pain.

"It turns away the polio. In the sack I sew myself. I get the Briosci. For eating too much. Maybe it helps."

No one should be awake at four in the morning, thought Joey, least of all his mother, who sewed little girl's dresses for fifty cents each in the steamy and dusty factory across the street on 18th Avenue. After downing the foamy remedy, he yawned and, to ease his conscience if not his cramp, pretended to feel better, and convinced her to go back to bed.

107

When her husband, Enrico, left for work that next morning in 1943, Philomena went down to call Dr. Pilo from the corner pharmacy since they had no phone of their own. In the meantime Joey went to the bathroom to light a cigarette as a possible cure, but it didn't help. To ventilate the smoke, he moved the top and bottom halves of the obscure glass window to the middle, giving him a glimpse of the second-story tiny court on which opened the bathroom and kitchen windows of the four apartments. Seeing nothing of interest out the window, Joey, sixteen, stood in his bare feet on the toilet seat cover to look again at the top this time. In the bathroom diagonally across the court, its window opened from the top, was Mrs. Pita, just recently married. She was washing with her cloth the back of her neck under her long dark hair, the dark hair under her arms, and her small pointed breasts. That was the limit of Joey's view. In those minutes he completely forgot that he was sick. Then he heard his mother coming upstairs.

He went back to his room to be sick again, wondering if the pain were self-induced to avoid his physics final. Up to now his scores were nearly perfect, and he might be a physicist himself someday, but the final exam, which made up a third of his grade, scared him to death. Maybe he wasn't as good as he hoped. He got in bed again to worry about that.

"The doctor's at the hospital," said Philomena. Coming in behind her was another woman, old, narrow, and dried up like a pepperoni in her red dress. Joey flinched at her red dress, since most Sicilian women favored black and other serious colors. Only the young ones at weddings advertised themselves in rose and lilac to attract the bees to the flowers. "Joey, this is Signora Strega. I call her. So we could do something. Before the doctor comes."

"Who's she?"

"When you had the tapeworm. You don't remember? She put the garlic on your belly. Under the teacup. Then it comes out," said his mother.

"That's baloney, Ma. You're smart. You don't believe in hocus-pocus. Magic doesn't work."

"Be quiet now, Joey. And listen. And lie down."

"I have to take a leak."

"Later. And watch your tongue."

The witch bared Joey's belly while keeping his modesty. With two stalks of celery from her brown paper bag, she constructed a flat cross, locating its center on his belly button. "Soon you feel better," said her wrinkled mouth. "No speak. And not your mother. Only me."

Joey pleaded with his eyes for his mother to release him from this witchcraft. Philomena was sitting on his brother's now vacated bed, and wasn't in charge for the first time in her life. "This lady's doing something funny here," he said.

Signora Strega, in red down to her stockings and shoes, with long ears that seemed to be melting on her head, sat in the chair and said, "*Silènzio,*" and sprinkled on his chest and belly the dry herb whose smell Joey recognized as basil for tomato sauce.

"I feel better," he said, faking.

"Go away, pain. Go away, devil. Go away, sickness," said Signora Strega, her tattered eyes closed, her head bent as if in her cupped hands the universe waited to obey her commands. "Joey, be strong, be healthy, be a fine boy. *È eccellènte. È stupèndo. È magnifico.*"

The flat of her hand touched his chest, then his belly, and then under his pajamas his thighs, just brushing by his penis, which he was afraid she might grab and put in her purse. Then her voice dropped to husky mutterings that Joey couldn't make out, and he listened instead to the buses clearing their throats outside his window, and to the honking cars, and he thought the test would have been easier to endure than this crap.

"True? You feel better?" said Philomena, unable to restrain herself.

The pain really was going away. Joey refused to believe that the witch had anything to do with it. Still, he forced himself to be truthful for his mother's sake. "Yes. I feel better."

"Signora Strega is a saint," said his mother.

"It ain't her," said Joey. "Sooner or later a bellyache gets better."

"Now I make the circles," said the witch. "One for each year. When I make the number sixteen, you get up. Then no more pain. Now I make the number one." She joined her thumbs and her palms floated in a tiny circle over his belly. Then her hands flew in enlarging circles until the last circle sailed on the waves of his hair, skipped on the windowsill, tickled his toes, and brushed at the tip of Philomena's strong nose.

Whether it was because Signora Strega commanded him to do it or whether he just wanted to be rid of her, Joey himself wasn't sure as he sat up in bed. Then he went to his chest of drawers for clean underwear and socks.

"Now you kiss the signora," said his mother.

"Do I have to?"

"You must."

The old woman's chin was growing a few black hairs, but, anyway, he kissed her red-painted cheek smelling like dried flowers. To swap what he thought was her bitter taste for a sweet taste, he kissed his mother's cheek too. Then he went to dress in the bathroom, smoking another cigarette stolen earlier from his father's pack. By then Mrs. Pita was gone from her sink.

A few streets away Joey's grandmother, Lillian, in her robe and slippers, was indecisively leaving her bedroom. Finally she descended the narrow stairs in her old house to prepare the breakfast tray quickly so as to limit her minutes away from her ailing husband. In that brief time she thought his thoughts, as if two minds became one from lying together so long in the same bed, and his thoughts chilled her bones. The knife in her hand, as she sliced her own baked bread, was the devil inviting her on a journey, but at her age, and forever toughened by steerage, she cursed the blade and, as if with disrespect, she put the knife away uncleaned.

In their bed upstairs Giuseppe Irprino was getting ready to die. Not that he felt sick enough to die. His pneumonia affected him only with high temperatures and slightly diminished breathing, but otherwise he wasn't uncomfortable. Up to this point he had been as durable as the boat hulls he built in the Brooklyn Navy Yard, of wood in his early years, and then of steel plates as strength took the place of grace. Never seriously ill before, he saw himself now as a burden for his young man within as well as for his off-center leathery old body, and without too much regret he looked forward to a very long night's sleep.

At eighty-eight Giuseppe was weary from doing the same things over again, weary from the same quarrels of his children with their spouses and their children, weary from the same summer heat and the same winter snow, and weary from eating and eliminating.

His one regret would be to leave Lillian. He would miss her, and would tell her that when she came back with his morning coffee. He would also say that his wine press was to go to his namesake, Joey Irprino. His grandson had cranked down the press the last few years when they made muscatel together and, unspokenly, they came to know each other.

They were men from different centuries, different countries and different educations, one exhausted and the other insatiable, but they met at the midpoint between them as if they were one and the same man, past, present, and future. He would miss Joey too, and Joey would mourn and forget him, as young people can forget even their own faces and be surprised by the mirror. But would Lillian forget? Could he leave her? Was it fair?

Then the hand of God reached up from his stomach to squeeze his chest, not with force nor malice, unsuitable to Him, but in the way Lillian could suddenly take his hand as she denied by her grip that they could ever part. And now, without thinking to call her, he did. "Lillian. Lillian."

His voice lacked urgency, but in the kitchen the cup fell from her hand as she grabbed her robe's skirt to drive her knobby legs up to their bedroom. There she threw off her clothes, and in bed took her husband in her wrinkled arms, and his breath rose like their canary to the top of the cage, and then dropped as if to the paper, and rose again.

Worrying that her embrace restricted his breathing, she backed off, but then his face soured, so she held him again. He knew she was holding him, and he had time only to say her name once more, and then he was dead.

Giuseppe was sorry he was dead. Lillian was still holding him, but he couldn't feel her nakedness now, he couldn't feel anything, yet he seemed to know everything there was to know. He knew that God played the mandolin, that Mary was a prude, that tomato sauce in heaven was cooked without garlic, and though the angels had dimples and nice legs they wouldn't dance with an old Sicilian. He wanted his old wife again, having lived with her for so long it was as if they were born on the same day. He saw in her face now all her ages from her birth to this minute, and he was lonely for her even though he was allowed to remain with her now. And Lillian held him all that day until evening when Joey's father came to visit *his* father. And then Enrico had to separate his parents, had to separate the living from the dead.

Joey thought he could buy his own suit for the funeral. "I wouldn't pick out purple," he said to his mother.

"But who sees it fits? It looks good? The salesman? You think he says the truth? Are you his son? He doesn't care if you go out in the laundry bag," said Philomena.

So the next day Joey and his mother hurried to the stores on 86th Street while his grandfather was laid out on the marble slab and embalmed, bathed, shaved, and dressed, to be returned in his mahogany casket to the parlor in his house for the next three days.

"Not a heavy one this time," said Joey, remembering that his confirmation suit was advertised never to wear out.

"We see," said his mother.

"How about Steubbin's?" he said.

"We look. But I don't like them. They don't give you a bargain."

"They have fixed prices, Ma. Like the A&P."

"They should want my business," she said.

"Suppose I also get a sports jacket? Leone has a sports jacket. We're going to New York for jobs in the summer. We don't want to look like hoods from Bensonhurst."

"We don't show off. Be like your father."

The salesman said, "You have broad shoulders. Try this on for size."

"Only black," said Philomena.

"We have a worsted navy in single-breasted."

"I don't like it," she said.

"It's almost black," said Joey.

"What size is the waist?" said Philomena.

"Thirty-two," said the salesman.

"You want to take in two and a half inches? Kill the whole shape?"

"We'll have the tailor take a look," he said.

"I don't need your tailor. I sew myself."

"I have a nice plaid," said the salesman, as they were going out, but they crossed the street to Kaufman's.

Philomena went to the rack herself and thumbed through the suits and found a black one. She held it up for Joey to look at, but he just dropped in the chair as if the fight that hadn't been fought was already lost.

"Mrs. Irprino," said Mr. Kaufman.

"You sold us the suit for my husband. But we paid too much."

"Even you should go downtown to Abraham & Strauss you won't find a better bargain than here."

"We see. This suit. How much?"

"Double-breasted isn't for him. He's a young man. And not so tall. You have to keep up with the times. In black he'll be a gangster."

"The men in my family wear black," said Philomena. "Double-breasted."

"You can have it. But first, let me try something. Just see this. What I'm doing." Mr. Kaufman whipped out a jacket, dark blue and single-breasted, and put it on Joey's back. "It was made just for you." Before allowing for contradictions from anyone, or allowing Joey to see himself in the mirror, he danced Joey by his shoulders to his mother, and she was the first to say whether she liked it.

"How much is it?" she said.

"Twenty-three ninety-five."

"It's made out of gold?"

"One hundred percent virgin wool," he said, now dancing Joey to the mirror. "Some handsome devil. God should have mercy on the girls when they see you in this suit."

"It's a little loose," said Joey, liking Mr. Kaufman even though he was pushy, since he was on his side.

"Go put on the pants," said Mr. Kaufman.

When Joey returned, the tailor was waiting with his chalk and pincushion. "You have the face that could be Jewish," he said. The small tailor was like an old baby, hairless and a little paunchy.

"Can you tighten it here?" said Joey.

"So see. I'll mark it with the chalk. To move the buttons. Then you'll be a darling boy. Your mother should give you such a hug. Now let me see the pants. You should do me the favor. Step on the stool. So I should see the cuffs. How they look. Since I'm not such a big person either. You know what I do? Look. No cuffs. They make you shorter. It's better not to have them. For me. One way or the other. It doesn't matter."

"Okay. No cuffs," said Joey.

"He's not short," said his mother. "He should have the cuffs. Like his father."

When Joey thought it was agreed that this was his suit, that it fit good, and that his mother had retreated from her objection to the color, she went to the rack again and took out another suit, black, but this time single-breasted.

"It's reprocessed wool," said Mr. Kaufman. "That's why it's a few dollars less. With the war on. You don't find too much virgin wool. It goes in the Army."

"You should make a better deal, Mr. Kaufman."

"So what's a better deal?" he said.

Now Joey understood the real reason his mother was here: to do the bargaining. She was never satisfied until the price came down. Now Mr. Kaufman looked at the label inside the jacket which was still on Joey's back, and then at the ticket on its sleeve.

"So five months. We have this suit in stock. So we bought it a little cheaper. So I'll give you the benefit. I'll give it to you the same price. As the reprocessed wool. Twenty-one ninety-five. You want a bargain? So that's a bargain."

"It's made cheap," said Philomena, pushing and pulling the fabric so that Joey inside felt like kneaded dough, shaking her head over the lining, breaking off a few threads hanging from the seams, and frowning in despair over the mess she inferred the jacket was in.

"It's a beautiful piece of goods," said Mr. Kaufman.

"Joey, take it off. We go someplace else. Down the street. To what's his name? H&M. Now *they* have suits. I know Hyman there."

Joey whispered in his mother's ear, "I'll pay the two extra dollars myself."

"It's the point," she said. "We should get our money's worth. It wouldn't be fair to pay his price. Mr. Kaufman expects it. It makes him happy to bargain."

"My last offer," he said. "I don't know why I'm doing it. Please, you shouldn't tell my partner. Give me $20. Take the suit."

"It's still too much, Mr. Kaufman." Now she pointed her finger at Joey. "I said take off the suit."

"You're making a mistake," said Mr. Kaufman. "It's made for your boy. Makes him look like a mensch, a man, God bless him. He should have lots of sons."

When Joey came out of the dressing room, two stone faces were waiting.

"Put it aside," she said. "Maybe we come back. If we don't find something. And thank you very much." Then she was walking to the door and Joey followed like an unwilling donkey and Mr. Kaufman followed him.

When she crossed the threshold, Mr. Kaufman, seemingly going down for the third time and short of breath, said, "So what do you think you should pay?"

"I give you $18. The waist fits. So you save on the alterations."

Mr. Kaufman took his pencil from his inside pocket and did math on the back of his business card while Philomena looked calmly at other suits on display, and then she brushed nonexistent dandruff from Joey's collar.

"So what's what?" she said, acting exhausted.

"The best I could do. This is my last price. If you don't want it, that's fine. Go to H&M. It's nineteen-fifty."

"Go write it up," said Philomena. "But absolutely, we must have it tonight. My father-in-law's coming home from the funeral parlor. Joey has to see him. He has to dress nice."

"Boy, I really want that suit," said Joey, relieved the bargaining was over.

"You should wear it in good health," said his mother, touching his face.

Joey was sick of dead people and had secretly made a promise to himself not to look another one in the face again, but his grandfather had been kind so he had to break his promise. All the other dead bodies had also been dressed up in their caskets in their parlors—his mother's father, two uncles, one aunt, a great-uncle, the landlord, his father's boss, his own friend, Frankie, who was killed on his motorcycle, three other related people he didn't know, and the first one, his playmate and cousin, Marguerite, with golden curls like Shirley Temple's, who at seven was laid out in her communion dress and looked like a plaster doll in her white box lined with white silk.

When he was going up the outside stairs he heard his aunts, and they made him pale and gave him gooseflesh. In the parlor his aunts, his grandmother, and his girl cousins over sixteen were all in black dresses, and the older women were screaming and throwing themselves on the body in the casket to hug the dead man who ignored them all. That was the way his grandfather was, he was moved only by what was inside of him, not by what others tried to heap on him.

The air was sweet from the carnations, roses, and gardenias in the shapes of crosses, hearts, and wreaths, all in a semicircle around the casket, which was on the stand against one wall. And the candle in the red glass in the man-size brass candlestick burned at the head of the casket as the prayer to the God who was getting back one worn-out soul and a handful of dust.

Giuseppe's leathery hands were folded over rosary beads, which hadn't happened when he was alive, since his religion at his nearly antique age had come down to his wife. He had always loved her, he told Joey that once, but had neglected her when there were other things to do—his work, his friends, his children, his wine, his garden, and his money—but then none of that mattered, and his wife, who was always there and had pained him in only the smallest ways, and had endured for him like the sun, was the one person he hadn't tired of, and now her grief rattled the walls and stung Joey's ears.

Since Joey's family was the last to arrive, his mother took her turn at throwing herself on the body in the casket to kiss Giuseppe's face, and the casket wobbled, so two uncles went to steady it. Then Joey's father said to him, "You the first son. So go to your mother. Don't cry." For a moment Joey wondered who was going to help him since his mother's screaming froze his soul, but his father's hand on his shoulder unfroze it. The women were doing the mourning for everyone—themselves, the men, not allowed to cry, the children, and even for their dead ancestors who would grieve for Giuseppe if they themselves were still alive. In the far corner was his grandfather's mongrel dog, Garibaldi, who understood only Sicilian and thought English was cat talk, and he was whimpering for himself.

With his aunts behind him, sobbing into the hollow of oblivion that had won out over life again, Joey, in his navy blue suit, went to take his turn at the bier, kneeling to say his *arrivedérci* to his grandfather. The corpse didn't scare Joey since it wasn't dangerous or evil or smelly, but was still and harmless. It was the same old man for whom tools performed, to whom women spoke with courtesy, and who could keep quiet when talking was noise.

Taught the physical laws of the universe, Joey wanted to believe now that in death the conservation of energy principle might also apply, as it did when trees became coal and coal turned into heat and heat was absorbed by other living things. Then his grandfather might be changed from an old Sicilian into bare earth, and earth into a tree, not just his molecules but also his spirit.

He was allowed to be alone at the bier with Giuseppe at this moment, while his many cousins were whispering and fidgeting and the uncles in their suits were standing along the sides of the parlor like silent shadows, perhaps preparing for the day when each would lie quietly in his own ruffled casket. So Joey's first words were prayers to speed his grandfather's soul to its heavenly reward, as always were said at the bier, but Our Fathers were insufficient now. Something more should be required of him in gratitude for his name, for the shared secrets of wine making, and for the press itself, his first grown-up possession.

Even his thoughts seemed inadequate, and because he had learned the art of swallowing his own tears before they could fall, crying too was a gift he couldn't give. Anyway, how did a guy speak to his dead grandfather? As though he could answer back? As though he were just a slain marionette up on its strings again in another performance?

"I'll go to the bay to catch your crabs," said Joey, inaudibly. "But I don't remember when to bottle the wine. You should've written it down. Or I should've. But you didn't say you were going. It's what good-byes are for. But I guess you had your reasons."

The room was suffocating from the closeness and heat, noises and scents, from too many sources, bodies and souls, flowers and candles, clothing and chairs. The light flickered unsurely, and the sunlight was unwelcome and held back by heavy drapes. In that cauldron, Joey could believe that his grandfather seemed to stir in his casket, as if the old man were amused at all the fuss, or had an itch he couldn't scratch with women watching.

Joey studied the powdered face, rouged cheeks, and blue lips and was convinced his grandfather's wicked smile was just under his skin, as when he had taken from his backyard coop a noisy rooster and twisted its neck in his bony hands for a Sunday dinner, and said that a man had to do hard things, had to kill the chicken to have its meat on the table. While Joey himself never expected to wring a chicken's neck with his own bare hands, he understood the lesson, but didn't know in what way he'd ever use it, and hoped that being a man was easier than that. But now his grandfather didn't speak, and soon Joey would have to surrender his place to his brother, Gino.

Finding no solace in religion in which he half-believed, nor in science which he loved, he could kneel there and generously despise death for its thievery. Then, hearing his father's throat cleared at the back of the room, perhaps as a signal, he stood up for the final kiss that he was required to give, placing it on the cold, smooth forehead that could have been a tin can.

Before turning away, Joey impulsively joined his two hands at the thumbs. He made the smallest circle over his grandfather's middle, and then successively wider circles over the body, until the last circle crossed the dead man's corrugated brow, and on the other end, his shined black shoes. In that room where hysteria was the air they all breathed, no one thought him any crazier than the others. Joey wasn't surprised, after the last circle, that his grandfather's soul was climbing out of the casket. His soul was clearly visible to Joey, who could see in his mind even such principles of physics as electromagnetism. Then grandfather and grandson were going out of the room together, side by side, one bent, the other with his ear cocked. Mackerel heads and beef trimmings would catch the most blue crabs in the square wire traps dropped in Gravesend Bay, the old man was saying, and at their heels was Garibaldi.

Guys Under Their Fedoras

When his father first sent him down to the basement under the pastry shop on Bleecker Street to mix dough for sesame cookies, Placido was fifteen, and he kept looking behind the 100-pound sacks of flour and sugar for the scratching rats.

"The rats don't hurt you," said his father, Leone Addomesticato. "But no trust the machine. It take you in the pot. Use your head."

Of more concern to Placido than the iron-corseted motors and the turning armatures were the creatures in the dark corners. At least once during each day's batch, when the dough mixer was still, a rat came out. For an instant Placido and the rat stared at each other like strangers on the Broadway trolley, possibly wanting to be friends, but each very wary.

A virtual prisoner in the basement to do grown-up work, as expected of many boys and girls in immigrant families in 1918, when child labor laws didn't exist, Placido at first resented his job. But later he was persuaded by his father that he was helping to pay their bills, and then he took some pride in his work.

When Placido's fellow prisoners, the rats, didn't bite him, he became used to their rasping, the muslin tearing, and their excavation of caves inside the flour. Not fearing them any longer, Placido began to think they were there for his amusement. If a bold one sprang out, as if a trap were mistakenly ejecting it instead of catching it (traps were tripped but always empty), he talked to the rat softly to gain its confidence. It wasn't fooled. Then Placido invented a game. Perched high on the full sacks and holding onto the light cord, he sat quietly. Confessional darkness and silence misled a few rats into leaving their hiding places. The light snapped on again, and they all scurried away like thieves when the black maria drove up at Washington Square Park.

When Placido tired of the game, he raised its ante by taking his father's six-shooter from under the cash register. With a handful of extra bullets, he again took his sentry post in the dark. After a few minutes, those rats daring to come out he shot dead. At that short range, Placido rarely missed. Every day he killed a few, until none was left. Taking the rats to his father, he collected the reward of a dime for each. They were then cremated with the trash in the backyard incinerator.

When all the rats were gone, the dough mixer with its slow monotonous humming was the only other thing pretending to be alive in the basement. Then Placido missed the secret noises, the unexpected gooseflesh as a rat appeared, and he was sorry they were all dead.

In 1943 the bakery lady, the library lady, and other shopkeepers had no part-time work to offer Placido's son, Leone, who had his grandfather's name, as was the custom, and now young Leone was before a storefront without a sign, the windows painted a dark green in which he could see himself. As he was going in, the bell overhead tinkled, but he had to wait. The young woman who finally came out from the back had blonde curls as round as his fists and breasts that bounced.

"What's on your mind, sonny?" she said, as if Leone had

some nerve coming in, since it wasn't really a store but a sparse office masquerading as one.

"Can you use a kid three hours afternoons? And Saturdays?" said Leone.

"This ain't no place for a kid," she said, propping her behind on the desk as if it took too much strength to hold up.

"I'm asking in all the stores," said Leone. "I put up stock for Bohack's, delivered capons for Hy's, and swept up for Nino's. Nino was teaching me to cut hair on kids. Then he got sick."

"So what's your name?" she said.

"Leone Addomesticato. I was born over on 16th Avenue."

"If a certain guy's here. I'll have to see. He might talk to you. Don't touch nothing."

The only things to touch were the desk, a couple of chairs, a typewriter, a phone, the *Daily News* open to sports, a cascading ashtray, and, for lack of water in their drinking-glass vase, daffodils hanging their heads.

The slim guy coming out from the back was wearing a suit the color of coal ash. His shoulders stuck way out, and his tie and handkerchief were bright blue like Leone's eyes (inherited from his father, the color surprised other Sicilian kids unsure if he really was one of them). The guy's black-band gray fedora looked brand-new. He almost looked brand-new himself, with a fresh shave and a black mustache so perfect it looked drawn on.

He lit a Camel. After inhaling, he acted as if he had made a mistake by not offering Leone one. So then he did. And Leone took it. The guy flicked his gold lighter, and Leone took a puff, and the guy took a puff. Then the guy grinned like a shark, as if Leone was a dumb kid trying to act older, but Leone took another drag, as if he didn't know what the guy was thinking, though he did. When he felt a cough coming up, Leone trapped it in his throat and knocked off his ash.

"Sylvia says you're looking for a job."

"For spending money," said Leone.

Sylvia, now sitting behind her desk, said, "This here's Mr. Anthony Tempesta. You know who he is? Most important guy around Bensonhurst. Around Brooklyn even."

Sylvia's introduction put a light in Mr. Tempesta's canceled eyes under lazy eyelids. Grinning again, he gave Sylvia's arm a little pat. Mr. Tempesta's teeth were blinding and he seemed to like to show them, and Leone was waiting for what would be coming out of his mouth. If the guy had a job for him, he was pretty sure it wouldn't be something easy like sweeping up curly locks.

"You smart?"

"I'm not bragging. I even skipped a year."

"Sicilian kids. They don't study. *Stùpido*. It's important you learn. Your father, what's he do?"

Leone told him his father was a pastryman like *his* father, but that *he* wasn't going to be a pastryman. He didn't want to sweat all the time by the hot ovens. Maybe he'd be a salesman and drive a new car.

"Let me ask you," said Mr. Tempesta, sitting, while Leone remained standing. "Who else's in your family? Where do you live? You have friends? A girl? You save your money?"

Leone talked for five minutes. He was sweating and going dry at the same time. Then Mr. Tempesta held out his hand. Leone went over and shook it.

"I like you. You talk," said Mr. Tempesta. "So far, so good. I consider you my friend. A Sicilian friend ain't somebody just to borrow four bits. He's a right arm. But it should be two ways. No?"

"Sure."

"Come in the back. You want this job—fine. If not—fine

125

too. Don't blab all over the street. You could make a few bucks. Like Sylvia here. Sylvia Cohen. You two could run this place. But first, we see. If you can see the good in what we do."

Since Mr. Tempesta was slim, he was fitting between the oil drums without soiling his suit. On the platform were two huge vats. A machine was attached to the workbench. Another machine was on the floor. And boxy cans without tops were against one wall stacked in a picture-book castle.

"You're in the oil business," said Leone.

"Your mother—when she makes sauce, the salad, what kind of oil she use? You know?"

"Olive oil," said Leone.

"Here we make the olive oil. We don't get it from Italy. With the war on. But we have to have the olive oil. So a little magic. To make the mamas happy. And we make the money."

Mr. Tempesta's fingernails, the dark ruby on his right hand, and his ruby cuff links sparkled. The hardest work he did, guessed Leone, was to flick his gold lighter. But now Mr. Tempesta surprised him by taking off his coat and tie. Rolling up his sleeves, he was putting on a rubber apron from his neck to his feet.

"You make the oil from olives?" said Leone.

"This drum. See what it says?"

"Corn oil."

"This drum?"

"Peanut oil."

"We don't use too much the soya," said Mr. Tempesta. "Pure soya, when it's fried, it smells fishy. When people use our olive oil, Madonna Mia olive oil, we don't want them having fishy oil. It says here on the can 100 percent virgin olive oil. Imported from Lucca, Italy. Virgin from the first pressing. So what we make has to be good as the label. So we mix up the oils."

"Isn't it against the law?" said Leone.

"Yeah. It is. So you want to go? Or you want to hear how we get the oil in these vats?"

"I want to hear," said Leone.

"We have the electric pump," said Mr. Tempesta, lifting a drum lid with a crowbar. "You pump half the corn, half the cottonseed, half the peanut, and a quarter of the soya. You do that for both vats. Then you go rowing."

When both vats were filled now, Mr. Tempesta handed Leone an oar and Leone stirred the oils. From the tin candy box with raised roses on the lid, Mr. Tempesta took out a cough medicine bottle. "This here's pure color. A guy in Jersey makes it. Start with an ounce. Then an ounce of essence from this one. Essence gives the smell, the taste. You stir again. Then you open the spigot. Fill the glass. Look at the color. Smell. Put in your finger. You should be tasting olives. Your mother—it's hard to fool her, no? That's what we have to do. Take care of nice Sicilian mothers unhappy without olive oil. I take it home to my own mother. My own wife. They think it's smuggled in from the old country. So how old are you, Leone?"

"Fifteen last Tuesday. You want me to get working papers?"

"Don't worry about that. I just care you're a good Sicilian boy. Come from a good family. And got the smarts. The guy did this job, he drives a new car now. In a nice suit. I never had nobody your age. But I need a hand. And you need a job."

"I want the job," said Leone. "Show me the color, and the smell, and after I try it a few times I'll get it right."

"Under the machine's a jar of Madonna Mia. That's your

127

boss. Your fresh sample has to match. You can make beautiful oil if you want to get it perfect. Even better than the genuine article. You think you could care about olive oil? About me? My friendship?"

Leone was thinking that Mr. Tempesta was a crook. He was a very likable crook, very spiffy, very polite, but Leone's father couldn't stand a crook. So Leone had a problem. He wanted the job, not to be a crook himself but to make a few bucks. He thought that since Mr. Tempesta could fool his own mother and wife, maybe he, Leone, could do the same with *his* mother and father. After all, his mother was still buying olive oil in the store and it probably was the same as he would be making.

Placido learned four recipes, and was thereafter charged by his father to make them as needed to keep each cookie pyramid stacked to its point. Soon, though, the job seemed to Placido as mechanical as the brass blade turning in the dimpled copper pot, always in the same endless circle within a circle, the blade rotating like the earth as it also traveled in the circle of the year.

Placido wasn't even able to read *The Call of the Wild* in the basement, for the dough had to be tested frequently and the machine switched off at the exact moment. Anyway, the bare light bulb, unless Placido sat high on the sacks close to it, would hardly illuminate the printed page. The basement in shadow, however, with the machine's jibberish drowning out the rest of the world, could be a place for remembering.

So Placido thought of Gina, so lithe, with clear egg-white skin. His friends teased him—told him he was too young for the silk-stocking women at the Palladium on Broadway. But with his quick blue eyes, dark hair brushed straight back and glossy with pomade, and in his father's black suit, he might soften a woman's red mouth when he looked at her, and she might even dance with him. Placido iced his cakewalk with sugary swirls, and his tango with Gina was almost a sin. Gina, a day nurse, took him to the fifth-floor walk-up on Elizabeth Street that she shared with Ruth, a night nurse. He played strip poker with Gina and he stayed all night. Widowed at nineteen when her husband of nineteen was killed in the Argonne Forest in the war, Gina had said, "You can stay, Placido. You don't ever have to go."

Punching the butter and egg-yolk yellow dough in the solid warm bubble, he remembered that night. Absorbed in his thoughts, Placido was forgetting to be on guard against the machine that could turn on him if he failed to pay attention. He was standing against the dough mixer's copper pot, his sleeves rolled up as a precaution. The blousy silk shirt was his father's, and was his gift, which Placido knew he shouldn't be wearing now, but it endowed him with an additional layer of manliness that he strongly desired for himself. As he leaned into the pot to punch, the excess cloth at his shoulder caught on the rachet nut locking in the blade. The sleeve had enough space for twice Placido's bicep, so he didn't quickly realize that the slow-turning blade was winding in the cloth. Even a second later, his arm pulling in, he wasn't alarmed and didn't call up to his father. He simply tried to unknot the fabric from the nut, trying to save his shirt. But the noose was getting tighter, until his shoulder muscle was against the rachet nut. Then it was dragging him in against the machine and around in the circle with the dough. His flesh tearing, his howling finally pierced the machine's muttering, and his father, rushing down, shut the switch.

The hole in Placido's shoulder fit his two fingers to their first joint. He bit his lip to subdue the pain and stifle his cry, but his father wept as he hugged his son to his chest.

Filling gallon cans at the spigot, Leone set ten of them on the workbench, dealing each a lid. Then he pulled the lever on one can at a time. The machine squeezed the lid and the sharp edges together. After sealing one hundred cans, Leone went to take a break and a smoke with Sylvia, but stopping in the doorway he listened. Two guys were in the office. One was shooting off his mouth and Sylvia was saying she didn't know where Mr. Tempesta was. Hiking her shoulders back, she bounced her breasts, but her breasts had no effect on the un-friendly guys under their fedoras. The big one with the cigar was a volcano. The one with the baked-ham face saw Leone in the doorway and, coming by, chucked him under the chin, sending a chill down his spine. That guy looked in the back room and then went out front again.

Leone kept watching. He didn't want them beating up Syl-via, but she didn't seem to be scared. She lit a cigarette, and the mountain said something in Sicilian. Then they left and Leone went into the front room.

"Hey, kid. You ain't worried?" said Sylvia.

"Nah," he said.

"Ain't nothing to worry about," she said. "Tony and his brother, Joey. They don't take nothing from nobody, if you get what I mean. Nobody's hurting a hair on your head, even if I have to plug them myself."

"You don't have a gun?" said Leone.

Sylvia opened the center desk drawer and took out a big automatic, silver like his mother's candy dish. She pointed it to the space where the guys had been standing and said, "Bang, bang." Then she put it away.

"Who were those guys?" said Leone, a shiver in his back that he would deny having.

"Guys that should be saying their prayers, once I tell Tony," she said.

Then she put her fingers in Leone's hair, as if he was her kid brother. He thought it felt very nice, so he moved in closer.

"Sylvia, you're beautiful."

"Your hair's so wavy. Wish I had it. What I have to go through for these curls. Want to touch my curls? Don't they feel nice?"

Not until Placido shut off the dough mixer did he hear his father's voice upstairs, not directed at him or at Placido's mother, Carmella, in their apartment behind the shop, but to someone in the store. Then Leone's shouting stopped. Placido waited to see if it would begin again. If it didn't, then he could continue his work. His shoulder was scarred, but otherwise he was as strong as before. He was making macaroons today, his own favorite, and he put in extra almond paste, mealy and toothaching, just because he ate them. Now his father's trombone voice came again, not in fear, only partly in anger, mostly as a command, indistinct but indisputable.

Placido would find out for himself what was going on. At the top of the stairs was the short hall separating the workshop from the store. Placido held back in the hall, watching his father behind the counter, a short muscular man with a face and head a few sizes too big, like a caricature of himself. His father was telling two guys in double-breasted dark suits and spotless fedoras to get out. Placido thought he would like to be as well dressed someday, but not as fat. His father was speaking in Sicilian. Placido usually understood Sicilian, but spoke it only brokenly himself. Of the two guys, one spoke and one didn't. The one who did was whispering, as if what he was saying was so terrible no amplification was needed. Placido couldn't make out exactly what he was saying.

The talking stopped. A quiet space like a big round table was between Leone behind the counter and the guys out front. They seemed to be waiting for a sign from Leone, and when it didn't come they whispered together. Leone thought he had won the argument. For his final blow, he was calling them "*il vile traviatóre,*" filthy rats, and ordering them out.

Leone hadn't won. He had only convinced them he wouldn't pay protection money to vermin and spat on their threats. So now each guy picked up a wire chair by the tiny marble tables where evenings Placido served espresso and spumone to customers, and using the chairs like sledge-hammers, they began smashing the glass cases. Their suits didn't wrinkle and their fedoras didn't slip off their heads as the glass shattered in shards on Placido's cookies and Leone's pastries.

Placido thought that his father had underestimated the danger of rats as he himself had the machine. He was a little afraid, as once he had been in the basement, but if it was necessary now, he would stand by his father and fight these monster rats.

Leone, disbelieving that two-bit gangsters were destroying his business before his eyes, seemed caught by surprise and momentarily incapable of responding. They were coming now, the chairs raised over their heads destined for Leone's own curly fringed head. Then Leone felt his son beside him, heard him say softly, "Papa, watch out."

From under the cash register, Placido grabbed the long-barreled pistol, but his father wrenched it from his hand. Then Leone, his chin stuck out, shot both guys in their wide lapels. The cracks from the barrel weren't muffled as in the basement by the soft sacks, but were swelled out into thunder by the hard walls and showcases. As the guys fell forward on the floor's small white hexagonal tiles, now in a red wash, their fedoras finally flew off.

Leone became the hero of his Greenwich Village neighborhood. Gangsters didn't come around to collect protection from shopkeepers on Bleecker Street for years. By the time they did come again, Leone had moved his wife and son across the East River to Bensonhurst in Brooklyn.

"You make the best olive oil we sell for two years," said Mr. Tempesta. "Your nose should be big. A small nose shouldn't smell that good."

"I use a little more corn. A little less cottonseed," said Leone.

"You have a dollar in your pocket?"

Leone took out two quarters.

"Sylvia, lend him a dollar," said Mr. Tempesta. "I have a sure thing. You two. You bet on the horse. Two dollars on the nose. Piece of Cake to win in the fourth. At Belmont. That's your bet."

"I never bet on a horse before," said Leone.

"We walk up the street to Lorenzo's gas station. I show you who to talk to."

"Is he the favorite?" said Sylvia, putting the singles in Leone's hands. "Who's the jockey? I love that Atkinson. A cute little guy."

Leone and Mr. Tempesta marched under the BMT elevated with the train running over their conversation, sounding,

Leone imagined, the way the war did. When they went in the gas station office, four guys got up from their chairs. Two had been in the shop weeks earlier acting tough with Sylvia. To the four, Mr. Tempesta said, "This is Leone. He's my good friend." He put his arm around Leone's shoulder. The men nodded to Leone and sat down again. "Leone wants to make the bet. Leone, tell Ricci what you want."

"Two dollars on Piece of Cake. On the nose. The fourth race. I forgot the track."

"Belmont," said Ricci, a bookmaker, desolate and sallow, as if he had lost most bets, when the opposite was likely. He took the money and scribbled in his small pad. "Good luck, kid. Runs at 3:50. Hang around. You'll hear it on the radio."

"Some other time, Leone," said Mr. Tempesta. "The kid has to do a little something. He comes to collect. The horse comes in. At five." To the guys who weren't tough now, Mr. Tempesta said, "Nice to see you, Angie, Pepe. You guys should bet that horse. I got the straight dope. It wins."

Piece of Cake, a long shot, paid $48 for their two-dollar bet. Leone split $23 to himself and $25 to Sylvia, which included the two dollars she put up. Leone brought his money home and folded it under the saltcellar where his father put his pay each week.

"You didn't steal it?" said his father.

"He gave me a bonus. I made over a thousand cans this week," said Leone.

"I been thinking these months," said Placido. "How oil comes from Italy? With the war?"

Leone was explaining again that it was smuggled in, lying to keep his job, but hating the lie, for if it was found out, he would suffer the loss of respect from his father, who often talked to him man to man.

Placido just shook his head and said, "You don't work there

no more. It's finished. You're too young, anyway, to work the machine." Leone pleaded to keep his job. Then Leone's mother, Rosalia, squinting with thought, whispered in her husband's ear. Then Placido said, "Okay. You finish the week. That's all. And don't beg me no more. And stand up straight."

Brokenhearted, Leone didn't tell Mr. Tempesta or Sylvia the next day that he would be quitting. As if to leave them with enough stock on hand until he was replaced, that one Tuesday afternoon he canned three times as much, six hundred gallons. Filling the vats again, he mixed in color and flavor, so that tomorrow after school he could pack an equal number.

Tired, Leone went to the office up front. He sank into Mr. Tempesta's stuffed chair and sneaked a look up Sylvia's crossed thighs, seeing almost to where her garter was attached. Sylvia was putting red polish on her nails. Then he opened the tabloid to the pictures and captions in the middle pages. Betty Grable was in her bathing suit to show off her beautiful legs that had just been insured by Lloyd's of London for a million dollars. Air Force men shot down in the Atlantic had survived eleven days in a lifeboat by eating their leather shoes and leather belts. President Roosevelt was signing a paper at his desk with some other men standing around. Two cars were smashed head-on. Another car with its doors flung open was parked under the elevated, two guys slumping back dead in the front seat. The caption said they were Angelo Capone and Peppino Piscatelli. Leone swallowed a hunk of air that felt like a lead baseball in a home run to the pit of his stomach. Did Mr. Tempesta know his two friends from the gas station got murdered?

"Sylvia, those guys who came in here. Those ugly guys. You remember?"

"Yeah. It's a real shame, kid. But they wasn't family."

"Jesus. They got shot in the head," he said.

"They didn't have good manners. It's important to have good manners. What Tony always says," said Sylvia.

"They stood up. In the gas station. When me and Tony came in," said Leone.

"They came in here rude to a dame," said Sylvia. "But anyway, Tony did them a favor. Before they died he gave them the same winning horse."

"It says they were gangsters," said Leone.

"Yeah. They was. It's a real shame they got it," she said, blowing on her nails to dry the polish.

"Yeah. It's a real shame," said Leone, the bell ringing overhead as he went out. The next afternoon he didn't go back to can the batch in the vats. And on Saturday morning he didn't go in to collect two days' pay either.